FRANKLIN VERSUS THE POPCORN THIEF

THE CHRONICLES OF FRANKLIN: BOOK ONE

LEAH R CUTTER

KNOTTED ROAD PRESS

Franklin Versus The Popcorn Thief
The Chronicles of Franklin: Book One
Copyright © 2014 Leah Cutter
All rights reserved
Published by Knotted Road Press
www.KnottedRoadPress.com

Originally published as "The Popcorn Thief"

ISBN: 978-1-64470-000-6

Cover Art:
ID 41487519 © Vasilev | Dreamstime.com
ID 57576452 © Jita | Dreamstime.com
ID 30569437 © Camrocker | Dreamstime.com

Cover and interior design copyright © 2014 Knotted Road Press
http://www.KnottedRoadPress.com

Come someplace new…
If you'd like to be notified of new releases, sign up for my newsletter.

I will never spam you or use your email for nefarious purposes. You can also
unsubscribe at any time.

http://www.LeahCutter.com/newsletter/

ALSO BY LEAH R CUTTER

The Chronicles of Franklin
Franklin Versus The Popcorn Thief
Franklin Versus The Soul Thief
Franklin Versus The Child Thief

Tanish Empire Trilogy
The Glass Magician
The Desert Heart
The Ghost Dog

The Shadow Wars Trilogy
The Raven and the Dancing Tiger
The Guardian Hound
War Among the Crocodiles

The Clockwork Fairy Kingdom
The Clockwork Fairy Kingdom
The Maker, the Teacher, and the Monster
The Dwarven Wars

Seattle Trolls
The Changeling Troll
The Princess Troll
The Fairy-Bridge Troll

The Cassie Stories

Poisoned Pearls

Tainted Waters

Spoiled Harvest

Bloodied Ice

Contemporary Fantasy

Siren's Call

The Immortals' War

Circle of Air

CHAPTER 1

FRANKLIN'S ALARM RANG TOO DAMN early, as it did every morning. Still, he didn't dawdle, or indulge himself by hitting the snooze button. Instead, he got out of his narrow bed, pulled the tan sheets up to make it neat, then walked through the dim bedroom to his tiny bathroom for a shower and his weekly shave, scraping carefully against his dark skin for the few errant hairs.

Putting on his brown Kroger uniform, Franklin hummed to himself, pleased that his weekly workouts with the Ab-Buster were keeping him in shape, just like the man on the TV had promised. He didn't pull the shades of his bedroom windows up until he was ready to leave the sanctuary of his room: He never knew what kind of ghosts might be waiting for him out there.

This morning, though, his view of his field of popping corn was unobstructed by any ghostly visitors. He spent some time looking at the front stalks. He only had five long rows, twenty stalks per row, and each one was precious to him. Winds had been light the night before, and he didn't see any damage. Broad green leaves grew out evenly from the tall stalks, and nestled in between them were the fluffy tassels of the best popping corn in all of Kentucky.

Yellow corn, of course. Franklin didn't go in for fancy strawberry corn, or that black kernel stuff. He grew grade A, American popping corn, using a hybrid seed that he'd paid good money for so it would mostly pop up into butterfly flakes, that were longer and more tender than the mushroom-shaped flakes.

And this year, he was gonna beat Karl Metzger, his old high school rival. Franklin's corn would finally win the blue-ribbon prize for the best popping corn at the Kentucky State Fair. He'd be able to hang that ribbon right there, above his dresser, between the pictures of his long dead papa and his recently dead mama. Make them both proud.

Satisfied, Franklin finally opened the door to his bedroom. He didn't know why the ghosts couldn't cross the threshold—maybe because no one but him had ever been in there, not since Mama had died, and she hadn't been in there that often. Still, he kept the door closed, as he didn't want to see their faces staring at him in the dark.

Sunlight beamed against the living room windows. The couch and overstuffed armchair lurked as dark shapes against the wall. It was gonna be a hot one today. Franklin left the shades down to give the house an edge against the heat. He turned on the ancient TV sitting on the even more ancient bureau to listen to the farm report as he made his way into the kitchen.

"Morning, Mama," Franklin said to the ghost sitting at his kitchen table.

Mama didn't say anything, as usual. She looked the same, her hair all done up nice, her good gold hoops hanging from her ears, wearing her best Sunday church dress. Being a ghost had faded out her black skin, brought out freckles across her nose that Franklin had never seen.

But it hadn't dimmed the glare that she frequently gave Franklin, like she did that morning.

Franklin tried not to take it to heart. He reasoned that being a ghost was hard on a body, particularly someone like his mama, who'd worked at the local beauty salon in town just so she'd have people to talk with all day. Not being able to say a word or touch anything—not even push a piece of paper across the table—had to be difficult.

"Corn's looking good this morning," Franklin told her as he got the peanut butter out of the top cupboard and the bread out of the breadbox sitting in the corner of the green linoleum counter. "I'll go out and check the fields when I get home. There's some weeds that need pulling." He got an egg out of the fridge, and reached for his lard.

He paused.

The cover of the mason jar wasn't tightly screwed on. It just rested there, with the lid seal off kilter.

"Mama, did you do this?" Franklin asked as he pulled the jar out.

She didn't reply.

"God—dang it!" Franklin said, unwilling to swear in front of Mama, even though she was a ghost.

Franklin had only opened that jar of lard last week; now, it was mostly empty.

Mama still glared at him.

This was Franklin's special lard, rendered down, white and pure from Sweet Bess, the pig he'd slaughtered earlier that spring. Sweet Bess had been anything but sweet. She'd been barely tame, rummaging in the woods next door for her food and only coming to the pen when the cold winter rains started. She was also a killer. Any chicken or small animal stupid enough to challenge her got eaten by her. This made her meat extremely sweet, smelling almost like perfume when Franklin cooked up her bacon.

Ghosts loved anything salty, would lick it up like a cat with cream. And though good lard would never go bad sitting out, Franklin kept it tightly sealed in the fridge.

So how the heck did a ghost get to it? He'd never met one who had the strength to open a jar. No ghost had ever haunted the refrigerator before, either.

"Mama, who was the greedy ghost?" Franklin asked, looking directly at her, hoping she'd give him some clue. "'Cause they ain't here now." All of the ghosts who haunted Franklin tended to stick around until he'd done his duty and helped them pass on, leave this earth and move to wherever it was that they was supposed to be.

Mama had never showed any intention of doing anything but sitting at Franklin's kitchen table for the rest of her death. She'd been sitting there for almost a year now.

But Mama didn't say anything, just glared at him like she did when he made a mistake that was, according to her, "too stupid for words."

So Franklin went back to fixing his breakfast—a fried-egg-and-peanut-butter sandwich. He screwed the lid on tight on the tiny bit of lard left and put the jar back in the fridge, hoping there'd be enough for his popcorn later that night. It wasn't corn he'd grown, he'd already run through that, and this crop had at least another couple of weeks before it'd be ripe. The first time he'd put Sweet Bess' lard on popping corn he'd nearly licked the bowl clean, but Mama had been staring disapprovingly at him from across the table.

He still didn't understand how a ghost had opened that jar. Or how it'd gotten into the fridge.

The weather report from the TV confirmed that it would be a hot one. Franklin finished his breakfast, washed his dishes, brushed his teeth, then got ready to go.

"I'll be home usual time, Mama," Franklin called out as he left the house. Then he stopped and checked over his shoulder just in case, but no one was passing by the driveway, which was open to the quiet street.

Not that it would have mattered—everyone in town already thought Franklin was crazy. Some of them even knew he sometimes talked with ghosts: Mama had bragged on him at the shop more than once. She'd always told him that it was important for him to do his duty to the poor folks who were stuck between worlds, even when it sometimes meant trespassing or asking strange questions.

From the front shed, Franklin got out his bike. He checked the chain, thinking that maybe that strong ghost had gone after anything greasy. It looked fine, though. No ghosts had messed with it.

Though Franklin could drive, cars were expensive, plus, he didn't like to take chances like that. If a ghost suddenly popped up while he was riding his bike, he could just fall over. In a car, he might hurt someone else.

Franklin didn't have to share the lane with any cars. He waved at Mrs. Wilkerson, out watering her geraniums, before he turned onto the bigger street. Here, he rode along the gravel edge, hearing his mama's voice, warning him how dangerous Stevens Road was. Cars whizzed by, nearly blowing him over.

But there was nothing for it. Franklin pedaled the two miles as fast as he could, huffing up the small hills, then coasting down the other side of the rolling street. The chorus of cicadas blasted him on either side. Fields of tall sorghum blocked his view of anything else, followed by neat rows of tobacco. The sky above him paled in the heat, with high clouds to the west.

From Stevens Street, Franklin turned onto the shoulder of the four-lane highway. Just as it narrowed down to two lanes, he passed by Metzger's Farm stand, with people already waiting in line.

Franklin pedaled by furiously. Everything that Karl Metzger turned his hand to grew bigger and better tasting than whatever Franklin tried. But Franklin was still going to beat him this year, get that blue ribbon prize for himself. His corn was growing well, and he had plenty of time to experiment with drying it, removing the perfect amount of moisture so each kernel would pop up tender with great wings.

The highway became Jacobson Avenue, and Franklin steered over to the sidewalk. Though he liked the shade of the trees, they also broke up the sidewalk, making it dangerous to ride along. Franklin tried to concentrate on it, and not spill over (again), but his thoughts kept going back to the ghost and the lard.

What was he dealing with? It must be a mighty strong ghost. Why hadn't it stuck around, to let Franklin know what it needed in order to pass on and stop haunting him?

As Franklin pedaled hard up Main Street, he shivered once, like something had just walked over his grave.

That ghost was something different.

And different was never good.

~

FRANKLIN DIDN'T MIND the tomato stains down the front of his brown Kroger uniform, or the dirt on his knees from kneeling to stock cans of sweet corn on the lower shelves. However, he'd also had to uncrate a box of that awful men's body wash, and of course, one of the bottles hadn't been sealed right. He could barely stand himself as he biked home as fast as he could, bumping over the broken sidewalks then along the four-lane highway, trying to create a breeze to blow the stink off him.

He didn't know if ghosts could smell or not. He figured they couldn't, though, so he wasn't worried what Mama would think.

If she'd been alive, she might have accused him of rolling in a back alley with some cat in heat, despite Franklin never having had a girlfriend. He couldn't imagine bringing home any girl that Mama wouldn't rip to shreds.

Franklin rushed into the kitchen, intending on going straight to the shower. "Mama, I—"

He stopped when he saw Mama had company.

Or rather, he had another ghost, sitting at the kitchen table with Mama.

None of his other visitors had ever dared. What made her special?

She'd been as black as Franklin when she'd been alive. He wondered if she'd worked with Mama at the beauty parlor 'cause she had bleached blond hair that curled softly around her face, the result of hours of work and product. Her once-bright red lips framed perfect teeth, and the color on her long nails matched her mouth. She didn't look much older than Franklin either, which was a shame—he hated it when people passed on early.

She also had some power, as she clicked those nails impatiently on the table, the only sound in the whole house.

Click. Click. Click.

Was this his greedy ghost from the night before?

Most of the time, Franklin only got impressions of what a ghost wanted, their *intent*. He rarely got a name, but hers came through, shining like her hair.

Gloria.

"Miss Gloria, it's nice to meet you," Franklin said. He would have been polite to her whether Mama had been sitting there or not—she'd raised him to do the right thing.

He didn't expect a reply, and he didn't get one.

"Is there something I can do for you?"

Nothing came, no hint of a place Gloria wanted to go to, or something she needed doing before she passed.

That surprised Franklin: Since her name had come through so loud, he'd figured her purpose would come as well. "Well, ladies, if you'll excuse me, I have to freshen up before dinner."

Both Mama and Gloria glared at him, as if this was too obvious.

Maybe ghosts did have a sense of smell.

If it had been just Mama, Franklin would have taken off his shirt in the kitchen and thrown it down the stairs to the basement right then. But that wasn't right, undressing like that in front of a strange female ghost like Gloria. So Franklin went back to his room to change.

Nothing was different there: The bed still had the sheets pulled up, his photo of Papa (who'd died when Franklin was two) and one of him and Mama still hung on the wall above his dresser, an empty space between them, where his blue ribbon would go. Franklin threw the offensive shirt into the laundry basket, then gathered up the rest of his dirty clothes. It was only Monday, and he generally did laundry on Tuesday, but this shirt couldn't wait.

He looked out at his field. He'd go pull weeds after he put a load in the washer.

Mama and Gloria hadn't moved from the kitchen table. They almost looked like mother and daughter, except that Mama would have called Gloria's shirt indecent. The top button was undone and it strained across her chest. If Gloria had worked for Mama, Mama would have made her go home and change.

Franklin started the washer, with extra vinegar for taking the smell out of the shirt, then eagerly went outside.

The air still held the afternoon heat, but the shade from the trees out back promised the coolness of the evening. The taller stalks of corn reached their heads up high to catch the last of the sun's rays. Scents of warm earth and growing things floated up to Franklin. The slightest wind set the corn to rustling.

Franklin looked out from his field to the land next door. It was sitting fallow, the For Sale sign weathered. The State Fair prize wasn't enough money to buy it, but maybe, with that money, he could talk Mr. Averson into lowering the price. Franklin had a bit saved, left over from Mama's insurance money—most of which he'd used to pay off the house, so he only owed taxes on it every year.

But wishes weren't fishes, like what Mama would say.

Franklin knelt down between the rows and pulled up some ragweed. He wouldn't ever spray—he'd heard too many horror stories of farmers ruining their food crop with the wrong weed killer. He made a note to get the long-handled dandelion digger later when he spotted a couple of those ragged leaves.

Franklin stood after a bit, wiping his brow with his kerchief. Weeding wasn't hard work, but it was constant. He took that as a good sign—everything was growing so well in his tiny field this year. He was sure to win that prize, finally.

A chill went down Franklin's back, not caused by any wind. When he turned, he jumped and took a step back. He hadn't expected Gloria to be standing so close.

"How can I help you?" Franklin asked. It was always best to be polite, especially with ghosts out in the corn field. They always gained strength there. Franklin had stopped going out into his field at night years before: Too many ghosts followed him there, trying to push their *intent* on him, enough so that he felt his skin turn sticky.

Gloria just glared at the stalks, as if somehow they'd done her wrong.

"Were you married to a farmer?" Franklin guessed.

Gloria shook her head. Sadness flowed out from her, like water from a broken hose.

Finally, they were getting somewhere. It was always a good sign when a ghost started reacting to Franklin: It meant they were looking for his help; that they might be thinking about passing on.

Mama had yet to react to anything Franklin said. He was afraid she intended to haunt him until *he* died.

"But you loved a farm—a farmer?" Franklin asked.

Gloria gave a hesitant nod.

Franklin sighed. This was gonna get messy. Ghosts with love on their mind were the hardest to satisfy. He hated this part of his duty to the ghosts, trying to figure out what a person that couldn't really talk wanted, who often wouldn't even respond when he did ask a question.

"Did he love you back?" Franklin held himself ready to bolt, but Gloria didn't do more than glare at him.

"So he loved you," Franklin said, relieved.

But Gloria didn't agree to that either. Instead, she shook her head at his corn and faded out of sight.

What did that mean? Had the farmer loved her? Or not?

And why did they have to come bother him about it?

Franklin sighed and returned to his crop, to the easier cycle of growing and watering and trimming just right, so much better than the complicated dance of the living and the dead.

THE NEXT MORNING, Gloria didn't return until Franklin was getting his bike out of the front shed. Clouds filled the sky, and the sticky air made Franklin feel as though he hadn't dried off after his shower. It would storm that afternoon. At least his crop was well enough established that unless it hailed, the stalks could withstand a strong wind.

"Good morning, Miss Gloria," Franklin said softly after making sure that no one walked on the empty lane out in front of the property. "Can I give you a lift into town?"

He'd done that before. Seemed like a ghost could ride on the basket, between the handlebars. Only two weeks before, he'd given a ride to a little girl (too young) with pigtails and a simple dress, who'd wanted a lift to the county judicial center just up the street from the Kroger so she could go harass the drunk who'd mowed her down.

Gloria took one look at his bike then raised one immaculately plucked eyebrow.

The *Are you kidding me?* came through loud and clear.

With a quick shiver, Gloria disappeared.

Franklin groaned. She was going to haunt him all day at the Kroger, he just knew it.

Was she strong enough to pull down a shelf? She was stronger than most ghosts, able to click her fingernails against the kitchen table. Franklin wasn't looking forward to finding out.

～

FRANKLIN COASTED his bike wearily down Main Street. The good news was that Gloria hadn't been strong enough to knock things off shelves. She was, however, a bad influence on kids. Somehow, just being near her was enough to make the younger ones cry and the older ones pick fights. Twice today, Franklin had had to stop teenagers from throwing cabbages or potatoes or whatever was handy at each other.

The storm promised by the dark clouds and heated air hadn't come. Wetness pressed down on Franklin as he cut across to Jacobson. He'd need another shower when he got home, though it wouldn't matter. He felt like he was riding through one already.

To lift his spirits, Franklin rode across Jacobson and up Stewart, turning north, heading toward what he called the sculpture garden. The Sorrels were from Los Angeles, come to his small town of Katherinesville to retire. Adrianna called herself an artist, while her husband, Ray, indulged her. She filled their yard with "found art": fallen tree branches wired together into tall, eerie men; pieces of glass collected from the highway and pasted together into stars; even plastic bags tied together and dyed, turned into colorful streamers.

Once a year, the Sorrels had a huge picnic. They invited all their neighbors and at least half the town to come and eat at their place. Tables ran the length of the yard, filled with fresh rolls, heaps of sliced ham, potato salad and coleslaw and corn on the cob and green beans and everything else neighbors brought to share, with ice cream at the end.

Gossip was that the Sorrels were some kind of Hollywood behind-the-scenes royalty. But they acted like regular folk—well, mostly—and if the gate door was open, Franklin would stop and chat for a while.

But the gate was firmly shut that afternoon. They did have a new piece hanging on the wooden fence, a strange metal cabinet with tiny plastic dolls pasted around the edges, framing it.

Was that really art? Franklin had no idea. He found beauty in his fields, in fresh growing things, in neat stacks of apples or well packed rows of carrots at the store.

And in the clean lines of kernels, after they'd been dried, ready to be popped.

Franklin headed north for a few more blocks. The houses were a mixture of old and new. Some of the buildings were colonial, made out of brick and tall, with many chimneys and clean, steep tin roofs. Some were more modern: rectangular and one story, from the '50s, like Franklin's. Green Kentucky bluegrass covered the yards. Despite the dry summer, purple flowering pawpaw trees bloomed overhead, brightening the day.

Just as Franklin had seen enough and was turning back toward Jacobsen, Gloria appeared, not two feet in front of him.

Though Franklin knew he couldn't hurt her, he still automatically swerved onto the grass edging the side of the street. His tires skidded, and Franklin fell.

"Dang it!" Franklin said as he stood up, brushing off his Kroger uniform. A green and black smear went down one pants leg. He was gonna have to do laundry twice this week if this kept up.

When Franklin looked up, Gloria stood unmoving like a sign post, one hand pointing away from Jacobson, up the street, farther into the neighborhood.

With a sigh, Franklin got back on his bike and pedaled the direction Gloria indicated. She appeared again, pointing him this way and that. Where was she wanting him to get to? How long was this going to take? His stomach rumbled. Not too long, hopefully.

Finally, Gloria stopped at the end of a dead-end street, in front of two ramshackle houses, and pointed to a trail going up between them.

Franklin shook his head as he got off his bike. It was bad enough that ghosts haunted his place. He hated it when they made him trespass.

But at least the houses looked dark, the owners not home. Trash lay piled up on the front porch of the one, with blue sheets of plastic covering the windows. Broken toys lay in front of the other.

Hopefully, neither of them had a dog in their backyard.

Franklin looked up and down the street. He didn't see anyone else there, waiting or watching. Damn it. He took a deep breath, squared his shoulders, and walked his bike up the trail Gloria was pointing to.

The backyards of the two houses were cleaner than the fronts. This was where the folks here lived, with lots of benches, chairs, and tables for them to gather at. They shared a long barrel smoker, and the smell of their recent BBQ made Franklin's mouth water.

Past the yards was a fallow field, full of brambles and sharp leaved weeds. Franklin pushed his way through, not bothering to untangle vines from the wire wheels of his bike. Hopefully no one minded his trespassing. Maybe, though, this would be the last of Gloria's haunting.

Finally, Gloria pointed Franklin toward a field.

Was this her farmer's field? Maybe he really could help her pass this afternoon.

Plus, corn grew in this field. Franklin happily walked into it. The stalks were tall, well groomed, and healthy. He judged the crop to be a little behind his rows: Maybe the farmer hadn't watered as much as Franklin had.

Gloria joined Franklin, marching angrily down the stalks toward a taller plant. Was there a particular place in the field that she cared about? Had something happened here?

Then Gloria stopped, holding out her hands in front of her.

Even from a few feet away, Franklin felt the wave of power that Gloria pushed out of her palms. She grew darker, less ghostly, as she pressed her will against a single ear of corn. But it wasn't hate that drove her, no.

It was fear.

What made her so scared of that corn?

Finally, Gloria got her prize, and a single ear dropped off the stalk and onto the ground. Gloria glared at Franklin, pointed at him, then down at the ear of corn.

Despite the heat, Franklin got a cold chill up his spine. He checked over his shoulder, but he didn't see another ghost. He scanned carefully, closely, but all he saw was more stalks of corn.

However, something else lurked there; a silent watcher. He just knew they weren't alone. A spirit haunted these fields.

With great reluctance, Franklin walked forward and picked up the ear of corn.

As soon as Franklin touched it, he knew Gloria's *intent*: She wanted him to steal this corn, steal all of this farmer's crop.

What had that farmer done to her, that she wanted Franklin to ruin his livelihood? It must have been real bad. If she'd been alive, she would have been shaking with fear. Something about this corn and this field scared her worse than any monsters could have.

"I'm sorry," Franklin said, as gently as he could. "I can't do it. I can't steal this corn for you. You're gonna have to find something else to help you pass on."

He'd never help a ghost to that extent. Not even if the person they was mad at had done something horrible. Gloria was just gonna have to find another way.

Gloria tipped her head back, turning her eyes up to the sky, then opening her mouth and screaming. Her face held sheer agony, like all the pinchers of hell was grabbing at her.

Franklin had never seen such a display.

Then Gloria marched over to Franklin and *pushed* at him, trying to get him to do her will, to leave all the stalks bare, dry, and leafless, like gravestone markers in the field.

"I can't," Franklin said, backing away, his skin feeling like it was being wrapped in sticky cobwebs. Gloria was strong, but no ghost was strong enough to force the living to their will.

Gloria stopped, paused, and gave a sly smile.

Suddenly, Franklin knew who owned this field: Karl Metzger, his rival for the Kentucky State Fair blue ribbon prize for growing the best popping corn. The man who had everything Franklin wanted. His old rival.

Franklin dropped the ear of corn he'd been holding like it was suddenly hot enough to pop all on its own. He raced with his bike along the long row and bolted out of the field, onto the highway, then pedaled like mad back toward town.

How could Gloria think he'd be so…so…dastardly as that? It just wasn't right.

Franklin would never do something like that, particularly not to a rival. He wanted to win that prize, wanted that blue ribbon so badly —but he'd do it on his own terms. He'd never stoop to cheating that way.

As Franklin got to his side of town, turning off the four-lane highway onto Stevens, the clouds opened up and blinded him with rain.

It didn't matter to Franklin that he had to walk his bike the rest of the way home due to the downpour, that Mama glared at him all through dinner, that he had to use the last of Sweet Bess' lard melted over his popcorn that night: he was content, 'cause he knew he'd done the right thing.

He also knew this was far from over.

CHAPTER 2

WINDS TORE AT THE HOUSE all night and thunder shook the trees. Franklin stayed in the sanctuary of his room, resigned to checking the damage in the morning. Mama had always told him that fretting didn't do no good. That night, Franklin tried to follow her advice, but his eyes kept popping open when the lightning flashed against his dark shade.

The next morning, clear blue sky gazed down on Franklin, washed clean from the rain the night before. Smells of wet earth and grass filled the air. Only Mama sat at the kitchen table that morning, her look less angry, more pensive.

All of Franklin's corn stalks had survived. They'd been knocked around a bit—the ground at the foot of a few of the stalks was loose, and they leaned forward a little, like a giant hand had been pushing at them—but for the most part, they were all good. He pushed the stalks back up and stomped on the wet earth, making it hold them more firm again. He plucked up a few weeds, pulling them easily out of the wet dirt.

Quiet wind rustled the leaves. Standing in between the stalks, Franklin couldn't see the house, or the yard—nothing but rows of corn. Peace filled him. He wished he could bottle it up and keep it with him when he needed it most, like the fireflies he'd captured as a boy, using them as nightlights for his room.

A feeling of stillness beyond the quiet of the morning told Franklin that he wasn't alone. When he looked up, he saw Gloria standing at the end of one of the rows. With a contemptuous hand, Gloria smacked one of his ears of corn. Power rippled from her, through the stalks and Franklin's chest.

Franklin rushed over to the ear Gloria hit. He didn't see anything wrong with it: It was still firmly attached to the stalk, not suddenly iced over or filled with bugs or some other nightmare that only ghosts could give him.

When Franklin looked back at Gloria, she merely pointed at him, her *intent* clear: This was merely a warning. More damage was on the way if he didn't help her.

Franklin gulped. "Miss Gloria, I can't steal Karl's crop. That wouldn't be right. It wouldn't be gentlemanly. There's gotta be something else I can do, that'll help you." Franklin wasn't gonna steal Karl's corn. Karl was his competitor. He didn't hate Karl. He envied him.

Gloria pressed her lips together tightly, but she didn't push any more *intent* at Franklin.

Her disappointment was obvious, though.

She disappeared before Franklin could say much else.

But what could he have said? He wasn't a thief.

LATER THAT NIGHT, after dinner, Gloria appeared in the kitchen again, sitting at the table beside Mama. Franklin wondered if they talked with each other in a way he couldn't hear, as they kept looking at each other, Mama with her hair up and her good church clothes, Gloria with her perfect blond curls, too-tight shirt, and long red nails that she kept clicking on the table.

They did seem to be in agreement about one thing: They kept glaring at Franklin, first separately, then together.

Well, maybe some more of Sweet Bess' lard would gentle Gloria.

Franklin went down to the basement, then stepped into the root cellar for another one of his jars. The darkness of the basement never bothered him much: He'd grown up seeing ghosts, having them give him nightmares. A little darkness wasn't ever scary after that. He liked how cool it was down there. Most of the basement had a concrete floor, but the root cellar's floor was dirt and smelled like his fields. A steep wooden staircase took up one wall, leading up to closed shutter doors. Deep shelves lines the walls, and Franklin had some spices hanging from the ceiling, gifts from his cousin Lexine.

Only a half dozen jars of plain rendered lard remained, along with some of the snow white, rendered leaf lard from around Bess' kidneys that he had stored in the freezer. He'd use the latter for making pies to bring to the Sorrels' picnic later that year, as it was pure and had no scent of pork.

Franklin hadn't planned on opening another jar so soon. He justified it to himself by telling himself that it was for Gloria. Maybe he could please her enough with that, so she'd figure out something else for him to do, instead of stealing Karl's crop.

However, neither Gloria or Mama seemed interested in the jar when Franklin held it up to show them. After cracking it open, Franklin approached the table slowly, so as not to spook Gloria. He didn't want her disappearing or going after his crop.

Inch by slow inch, Franklin held out the open jar for Gloria. Would she understand what he was offering?

Puzzled, Gloria sniffed at the lard, then curled her nose up at the smell of it and disappeared.

Damn it! Why didn't she want the lard? She'd certainly been going after it earlier.

Mama moved her hand from the table for the first time since she'd started haunting Franklin.

Startled, Franklin held himself absolutely still. What was Mama about to tell him?

Slowly, Mama raised up three fingers. *Intent* oozed from her, like butter melting over popcorn.

There were three ghosts haunting Franklin: Mama, Gloria, and another, unnamed, unseen ghost.

Mama was worried about her boy.

An unseen ghost haunting Franklin? That just didn't seem right. Ghosts haunted Franklin because they needed his help. They'd been doing it since he was a boy. Mama had always told him it was his duty. And he sure hadn't done anything to make a ghost want revenge or come after him.

Maybe the ghost was just ornery enough to haunt Franklin without wanting his help. But that still didn't seem right. And it wouldn't worry Mama, not that much.

What was this other ghost? And what did it really want?

ON HIS LUNCH break the next day at the Kroger, Franklin hurriedly ate his sandwich and went to find Charlene, the store manager.

"Hey darlin'," Charlene said, welcoming Franklin into the little security booth on the balcony of the store. "What can I do you for?"

The room held a half-dozen TV screens, all black and white, showing different places in the store, like the liquor coolers in the back, the two cashiers up front, and the baby and diaper aisle—they'd had a problem recently with formula going missing. Like the rest of the store, the room smelled like old wood and dust: The building was a turn-of-the-century store front, gutted and converted into a more modern store.

Franklin had never felt comfortable up there, spying on everyone. Charlene always struck him as a little too keen on security.

Charlene's uniform was a long-sleeved white shirt with the Kroger logo over her right breast pocket, black trousers, and a utility belt that rivaled any comic book character's. She cut her brown curly hair short and always wore what Mama called "work makeup"—just enough to make her pretty, but never enough to be noticed. Fortunately, Mama had never tried to set Franklin up with Charlene. Franklin had always assumed it wasn't because Charlene was white, but because of her size: She was taller and wider than Franklin (who wasn't a small man) and at least twice as strong.

"Figured I'd come and catch up on the local gossip," Franklin said with a grin, holding out his bribe: half a bowl of the fresh blueberries that had just come in, drowning in cream.

"You know I don't gossip," Charlene admonished as she took the bowl with one hand, while indicating that Franklin should sit on the other chair in her "command center." "Thank you," she added with a shy smile.

"Then maybe you can catch me up on the news," Franklin said.

"Well, you know the Whittiers?" Charlene started. "They live up near the big Baptist church, off Fifth. So Jimmy—you know Jimmy, the dry cleaner—he was saying…"

Franklin nodded, letting Charlene spin her tales. The problem wasn't ever getting Charlene talking, but getting her to stop. It was why he'd come to see her at the end of his break, not the beginning.

"So, have any bad people been killed on the highway recently?" Franklin asked when he felt he could get a word in.

"No, no, not that I could say," Charlene said. She put the empty bowl back on the desk in front of her. "You sure are a gruesome thing, ain't ya? Always asking about who's dying."

Franklin shrugged and tried to act casual. "Just an interest of mine," he said truthfully.

"The only big news we've had is that some big developer, a businessman, has gone missing. He was supposed to call into his office yesterday, on Monday, and didn't," Charlene said.

"What do you mean, missing?" Franklin asked, wondering. A developer—that might make a hungry ghost, particularly if he was looking to buy up anything in their little sleepy town.

"You can't say a word to anyone else," Charlene said, leaning forward and lowering her voice. "I heard it on the scanner."

Charlene kept a police scanner in her car, and sometimes followed Sheriff Thompson or went out to where there was trouble. Not that it was illegal, but the sheriff and his deputies didn't like Charlene much. She insisted it was because they were threatened she'd do their jobs so much better, if only she'd gone into law enforcement instead of business.

"I promise I won't tell a soul," Franklin assured her.

"So this guy—Jackson, I think his name is—came here to see about building a resort."

"Here?" Franklin scoffed. "There's nothing here." Katherinesville was a historic town. It had its share of colonial buildings, and the third floor of the eye clinic had been the old opera house and still showed plays. But it wasn't as fancy or preserved as the bigger towns, like Bardstown or Harrodsburg. The countryside was pretty enough, but so was most of Kentucky.

"Ah, but what if he diverted Wolf River?"

"Could they do that?" Franklin asked, astonished. What would happen to his taxes if the town became prosperous? Could he still afford to live there, or buy the property next to his? "I sure hope they don't."

"Well, that's just the gossip," Charlene said with a grin. "Anyway, he met with some of the local bigwigs, like the Sorrels and the county governor and the mayor. Then he wanted to poke around, get some of the 'flavor' of the area."

Franklin snickered. "Flavor. I'll say." Why did city folks think places like Katherinesville were so quaint? When Charlene didn't go on, he added, "So what happened to him?"

"He disappeared. Never made it to his plane. His rental car wasn't returned. He hasn't checked his email, or called into his office."

"Couldn't they find him on his phone or something? Triangulate?" Franklin asked.

"You been watching too many cop shows on TV. That only works if there's a signal. Can you get reception out in the middle of your field?"

Franklin shook his head *no*. He didn't have a fancy, smart phone —as Mama had said, those things made you dumb. But he did have a cell phone that he could use, when he remembered to charge it. But Charlene was right—it was useless out in the middle of his field.

"So they can't find him. Or track him. He's just fallen off the face of the earth. People are speculating that the deal he wanted to make went bad."

"Or maybe not," Franklin replied. "If he's really that busy and important, maybe he just wanted to take some time off."

"Maybe," Charlene said, nodding. "But I bet there's been foul play."

"Now who's been watching too much TV?" Franklin teased. He stood up and gathered their bowls. "I appreciate the news," he added. "But my break's about over."

As Franklin headed out, Charlene called after him, "You want me to tell you if they bring a fancy crew out just to track one man?"

"Sure thing," Franklin said, though he had a better tracking device than any of the equipment he saw on those shows on TV.

He had his cousin Lexine.

~

FRANKLIN TUGGED on his gloves and reached for the first head of red leaf lettuce. Stocking lettuce wasn't as bad as cleaning out the wet rack where the lettuces was displayed, even if he didn't like trimming leaves off the heads, particularly when they were slimy. He kept his knife sharp, so it was a bit easier.

But he'd forgotten to turn off the sprayer, so of course, the next time he reached back to set a head of lettuce in the wet rack his glove and arm all got wet.

"Dang it," Franklin said under his breath so no one else would hear. He didn't have any paper towels on his cart, either. He marched down to the end of the display and turned off the sprayer, then went back to break room to pat down his arm.

By the time he came back, Gloria stood there, smirking, as two brothers, Mark and Louis, flung stringy, slimy lettuce cuttings at each other.

"Mark! Louis!" Franklin bellowed.

The boys stopped mid-throw and looked guilty. "We're sorry Mr. Kanly, sir," Mark said as he realized that there were bits of slimy lettuce on the floor, as well as dripping off the front of the vegetable case.

"Don't tell our mom," Louis begged.

Franklin sighed. Luckily, he'd brought the paper towels with him.

"You go find her, then," he said gruffly as he bent down to wipe up the gunk on the floor.

The boys skedaddled. Franklin didn't feel too badly about them—they'd clearly been under the influence of Gloria. No need to warn their mother, Mrs. Mason. She already had enough on her hands, with four boys. His mama had always said that she was lucky she'd only had the one, 'cause she swore that more than one would have sent her clear around the bend.

Franklin finished cleaning up and had started trimming lettuce leaves again when Mr. Sorrel came up, a mere loaf of bread and a small pack of cheese sitting morosely in his wire cart. He wore a loud red-and-yellow print shirt with cartoon figures Franklin didn't recognize, beige shorts, white socks and sandals. His white hair was perfectly styled and filled his whole head, despite his seventy-plus years. He had a bland face, the kind you'd forget in an hour, unless he found you interesting and suddenly focused his gray-blue eyes on you and you'd realize just how smart he was.

"Good afternoon, Mr. Sorrel," Franklin said politely.

"You can call me Ray," Mr. Sorrel responded, as he always did.

And outside of the store, Franklin would. But not at work, where he needed to show more respect.

"So how've you been?" Mr. Sorrel asked politely.

"Can't complain," Franklin said, more or less honestly. He had a troublesome ghost, no, three, haunting him, but he still had a roof over his head and the best popping corn in the state growing in his backyard. "How about yourself?"

"I'm glad I ran into you," Mr. Sorrel said. "Your mama, God rest her soul, used to tell fortunes at the beauty parlor, right?"

Franklin nodded warily. "She had a tarot deck that she'd use. Or regular house cards, sometimes. It was just to keep the girls at the parlor entertained." Mama didn't have a gift, not really. Not like Franklin or Lexine.

Though sometimes, Franklin wondered. Mrs. Leslie had been a regular at the beauty parlor for years. Then she stopped going abruptly, and went the next county over for her weekly appointment.

At Mama's funeral, Mrs. Leslie came and cried on Franklin's

shoulder about how his mama had been right about everything she'd said, everything the cards had said, but Mrs. Leslie hadn't had the courage to go back.

"And you help people too, don't you?" Mr. Sorrel said, his gray-blue eyes suddenly piercing and sharp.

"I'm not sure what you mean," Franklin said, not willing to go into his business—particularly not here at the store. Who knew if Charlene was watching or not?

"People say you talk to ghosts," Mr. Sorrel said.

"People say a lot of things," Franklin replied, trimming another head, unwilling to just outright lie. Mama didn't like it when he lied.

"We seem to be having some kind of haunting at the house," Mr. Sorrel said. "Could you stop by tonight? After work? At least come by and say hello to Adrianna."

Franklin looked up from the head of lettuce in his hands. Mr. Sorrel didn't seem scared, at least.

"I can stop by," Franklin said slowly. "But I ain't saying anything to any ghosts." If Mr. Sorrel was being haunted, it was probably for something he'd done at some point.

Ghosts didn't just haunt people for fun.

FRANKLIN RESTED his bike against the wooden fence of the Sorrels' place. Nothing new had been added to the collection of art there, though the metal cabinet had lost a couple of doll heads, making it a little more creepy, with just the doll bodies framing it.

The doorbell next to the gate had been switched out since the last time Franklin had been there. The round, lighted button now sat at the heart of green-blue brass swirls, like a pearl at the bottom of the sea. Franklin pushed it gently, hoping that maybe the Sorrels weren't home and he could be on his way.

The gate buzzed and unlocked, swinging open almost immediately. Franklin debated leaving his bike just leaning against the fence, but he wanted to make sure it was still there when he left, so he pushed it through the gate and leaned it against the wall just inside.

Cheery yellow daisies made out of clothespins lined the white stone walkway. Children's pinwheels spun merrily beside them. A tall silver statue of a man, made from hubcaps, stood hunched next to the door of the low, one-story house, his arms extended, holding a hubcap filled with water for the birds.

Mr. Sorrel—Ray—came out the door. Adrianna floated beside him, wearing a dress made of white and purple scarves, like what Franklin had seen singers wear in music videos. The skirt flared out, like the cloth was lighter than air.

"Franklin!" Adrianna called, skipping over to him and clutching hold of his arm.

Normally, Franklin didn't care for folks touching him. But Adrianna, she was in a class not meant for other folks. Her hazel eyes shone clear today above her freckled nose, while her brown hair hung down loose and clean, past her shoulders.

"Good afternoon, Miss Adrianna," Franklin said, lightly patting the hands wrapped around his bicep.

"How you doing today?" Adrianna asked.

"I'm doing just fine," Franklin said. He couldn't help but smile at her. "How have you been?"

"All Ray's fish died again. In the koi pond, out back," Adrianna said. She gave a delicate shiver. "The water all ran out. Ray says there isn't a leak."

"No leak," Ray confirmed. "The plug keeps getting pulled."

Franklin didn't want to point out that it was unlikely that a ghost could have done it—not unless that ghost was real mad. Most didn't have the strength.

But a ghost like Gloria might be able to. Or maybe even his unseen visitor, the one strong enough to open a jar of lard.

Were either of them haunting more than just Franklin? Did Gloria have something against Ray, too?

"Why don't you show me?" Franklin said.

"Good!" Adrianna exclaimed. "I told Ray that you could help. I don't have the sight, not like you. But you have it, right?"

"Let's just see what we can see," Franklin said, not admitting nothing to nobody.

Adrianna tugged Franklin along the path, leaving Ray in their wake. "What do you think of the new design?" she asked proudly.

"New design?" Franklin asked, confused.

"The path! Now it follows all the spirit-power lines."

"Ah," Franklin said, looking down. New grass lined the edge. The path had been laboriously moved about two feet to the left. "Very nice," he said when it was obvious Adrianna was looking for a reply.

"See?" Adrianna beamed over Franklin's shoulder at Ray. "I told you we should do it."

"Yes, dear," Ray said in a long-suffering voice.

"He doesn't really mean that," Adrianna confided in Franklin. "He feels better walking this path as well."

"Yes, ma'am," Franklin said. It was always best to just agree with Adrianna. Especially when he didn't understand half of what she said.

In addition to the tree men wired together from fallen branches stood several other statues: A half-complete mermaid that Franklin guessed was pieced together out of found glass; what looked like a goat man, up on his hind legs, made out of balls of twine; a long streaming V of dark birds dangled from dark rope that linked one tree to the next; and a collection of outboard motors all painted blue and white, sitting on top of fancy pillars.

They curved around the yard, circling through the statues, before they reached the pond, a plain concrete ring about three feet deep, with just a touch of water still remaining in the bottom. It looked clean, was a pretty blue, and stank of dead fish.

"Where's the plug?" Franklin asked Ray. He didn't see any ghosts, but that didn't mean there hadn't been there earlier.

"Let me show you," Ray said.

Franklin gently rolled away Adrianna's hands and followed Ray as he stepped over the concrete lip.

The plug sat at the center of the bottom of the pond. It looked like an oversized bathtub plug, made of black rubber with a brass ring through the top of it and a chain. Franklin tugged on the chain, but it didn't come up easily. He tugged again, putting more muscle into it.

"You said the plug gets pulled up at night? This plug?" Franklin tugged again, finally getting the plug to release.

"Yes, almost every night," Ray said.

"It's the spirits, right?" Adrianna asked. "They don't like us trapping living things. I told you, Ray."

It couldn't have been a ghost. No ghost that Franklin had ever met had the strength to pull up that plug.

And he really didn't want to meet a ghost who had that kind of strength and will.

"We shouldn't trap live things," Adrianna said. "The spirits don't like it. Right, Franklin?"

Why was Adrianna staring at him like that?

But she was right. "Sprits don't like you trapping living things," Franklin admitted. It was why he didn't have a pet, not a hound or even a turtle. The ghosts would put a hole in the screen door for them to get out, push on any cage door until it was ajar.

"So it's the spirits pulling the plug," Adrianna said earnestly. "It must be the spirits. It can't be anyone else, right, Franklin?"

Franklin looked up at Adrianna, who kept staring at him, then back at Ray.

"You don't like the fish being trapped either, do you, Miss Adrianna?" Franklin asked gently.

"No, but Ray likes 'em. So it must be the *spirits* that want them free," Adrianna said again.

While Mama may have accused Franklin of not being the brightest bulb in the pack, even he could see what was happening here.

Adrianna was pulling the plug at night, and blaming it on ghosts.

"Now, Ray," Franklin said, stopping until the man looked at him. "Adrianna is right. Spirits don't like you trapping living things. Free spirits. Of all kinds," he said, glancing up at Adrianna, then back at Ray. "They might love you, but trapping living things make 'em kind of nuts."

Ray looked up at Adrianna and sighed. "Well, I'll be—" He

stopped, and paused. "All right. I hear ya. Free spirits will be free, and free everything around them, won't they?" He stuck his hand out for Franklin to shake, then lowered his voice to a whisper. "I appreciate your discretion in this. No one needs to know just how free a spirit Adrianna is."

Franklin grinned at Ray. "I won't tell anyone but Mama."

CHAPTER 3

DESPITE IT BEING HIS DAY off, Franklin set his regular work alarm, which still went off too damn early. However, he let himself snooze his alarm once before he opened his eyes and stretched his arms up in his narrow bed, touching the wall with his fingertips while his toes slid off the end. His Ab-Buster workout the night before had left him a bit sore.

Franklin jackknifed up, touched his toes, then flopped back down his bed again. Yep. He was sore. But a man had to stay in shape. Particularly when he wanted to look good in the photos for the local paper, when he won the blue ribbon prize for growing the best popping corn.

But today—today Franklin had to go see his cousin Lexine. She lived off in the woods, out where there was no cell reception, in a cabin she'd seduced one of the local contractors to build for her.

Some of the folks in town called her a witch, though never to her face, and never when Franklin could do something about it. She wasn't really a witch. She was just cleverer than most. She also saw spirits.

Franklin preferred ghosts to spirits. He always figured he could at least try reasoning with a ghost—after all, they'd once been human.

Spirits were what remained of dead animals and other creatures that Franklin had no name for, like the soul of a sad wind, or the remains of a burned-out mill. Still, Lexine did her best to calm whatever spirit came calling on her.

Mostly Franklin never saw spirits, and Lexine never saw ghosts. Their powers shifted only when they were near each other. At first it was uncomfortable, particularly as teenagers, but they'd both gotten used to it. Now they sometimes did it on purpose. Franklin would take hold of Lexine's hand and show her a ghost, share his vision with the only other person in the world who could see.

Lexine was a cousin through marriage only: An adopted daughter of Mama's older sister when she'd remarried. But everyone said Lexine fit right in with the rest of them.

Mama shared the kitchen table with Gloria that morning. And most of his newly opened lard was gone, too.

"Dang it! Mama! Who's doing this?" Franklin said, shaking the jar at her.

Mama wasn't glaring though, wasn't even looking at him. Neither was Gloria. They stared at the table instead.

Were they ashamed? Couldn't they stop the greedy ghost?

Franklin sighed. "It's okay, Mama. I just won't bring any more up, not 'til I settle this thing." He made a bigger helping of his special breakfast sandwich, since it was a good long bike ride up to Lexine's cabin: Three eggs piled high on top of a piece of bread slathered with peanut butter, and some banana slices as well.

"I'm going to Lexine's today," Franklin told Mama. "There's a businessman gone missing. Don't think she had anything to do with it, but maybe her spirits know where he's hiding at." Franklin felt positive that the man had just taken some time off, and would show up soon.

Both Mama and Gloria looked up at that. "Do you have a message for me to bring to Lexine?" Franklin asked eagerly. Maybe Lexine could help him, get either Mama or Gloria to pass on and stop haunting him.

But neither Mama nor Gloria said anything or pushed any *intent* at him. Gloria glared. Mama looked sad.

"You remember Lexine?" Franklin asked Mama.

Now she glared at him. Of course she did. Then her thoughtful look returned.

Franklin didn't know what that was all about. He was gonna have to talk Lexine into coming back here to the farm with him. Maybe this time she'd be able to see Mama. Even if she couldn't, he could translate, at least. Maybe Mama had something she wanted to say to Lexine. And maybe that would help her pass on.

Or maybe Mama just intended to haunt Franklin forever.

FRANKLIN GLADLY PEDALED SLOWER ONCE he got off the pavement and onto the dirt road, under the towering trees. It smelled clean like pine and dark earth. Broadleaf bushes grew under the tall trunks, along with brambles full of blackberries. Birds and crickets sang him along.

If Franklin could afford a place back in the woods here, he would. But he'd have to buy the land, and the easement, and probably a car to get himself to his job. Plus, he'd have to pay to have a hunk of the trees cleared out for a field, and then it would take a couple years to get the soil just right. Still, a man could dream.

A black SUV sat parked at the start of the driveway to Lexine's cabin. That was strange. Lexine didn't get many visitors. It was a rental, too. Maybe she'd gone ahead and put up that web page she'd always talked about, Spirits "R" Us, advertising her services.

But why was the car parked so far from the cabin? Had its owner just pulled off the road here?

Franklin took a long swig from his water bottle after he got off his bike, then wiped the sweat off the back of his neck with his kerchief. It was cooler under the shade of the trees, but the day was still hot, and the air was sticky.

The spirit of Sweet Bess suddenly appeared, standing between Franklin and door to Lexine's cabin.

"Shit!" Franklin exclaimed, ready to hop back on his bike and race out of there.

Sweet Bess, the two other times she'd appeared to Franklin, had tried to mow him down for turning her into bacon. She was the one spirit he could see without Lexine. The sow couldn't hurt him, but having a ghost or a spirit pass through a body made Franklin shiver for a day.

But the giant sow just tossed her head at him. If she'd been alive, he would have heard her deep grunt. Then she ambled away, back into the woods.

Franklin shook his head. He'd never understand spirits.

Still, the encounter left him unsettled. He approached the plain brown-wood cabin carefully. It looked the same as it always had, a one-story house, just one step up from a shack. Perfectly square, it squatted under the trees with a resigned air. The two front windows on either side of the red door were dark, with no shades—Franklin didn't think Lexine owned any.

As Franklin walked across the broken brick walkway, he noticed the front door was ajar.

It didn't seem like Lexine to leave her door open. Maybe she was expecting other visitors? Like the strangers in the rented SUV?

Franklin stepped across the threshold and called out, "Hello? Lexine? Anyone home?"

The only sound he heard was something buzzing, angry and frantic, coming from the left, where the living room was.

Franklin paused and let his eyes adjust before taking another step into the room. He was glad he did.

The place was a shambles.

Torn-up pieces of paper littered the wooden floor. The twisted rosemary plant that had guarded the door lay broken, its dark stems scattered, the scent pungent. The old couch sat skewed, pushed almost to the wall. Glass from the side window, not visible from the front, spread out in a spiral pattern across the wood, like much of the debris. The pictures hanging on the wall—old drawings of plants and insects—were torn and punctured, the holes aligned in a spiral. Lexine's desk had been turned over and lay on its side, like a dark wounded horse.

As Franklin went around the couch, he saw blood. Lots of blood.

Franklin rushed forward.

Lexine lay with her head at an odd angle to her body, like a broken doll, her dark eyes blank and staring. Deep slashes marred her arms and legs, like some kind of wild animal had been scratching at her, the blood long since dried. The angry buzzing came from the flies crawling all over her.

Franklin looked away, sickened. Who—no, what—did this?

Was it that crazy missing businessman?

Except that when Franklin looked up, he could see a pair of legs, not moving, on the kitchen floor.

Franklin made himself go and look.

It appeared to Franklin that the businessman—Jackson?—had been trying to get away from whatever the hell had found the pair of them. The white kitchen door held bloody fingerprints from where he'd broken off his nails, scratching, trying to get out. He wore a suit, so it was his face that was all slashed up, like from a knife-tipped rake.

Franklin looked around the kitchen. It wasn't in as bad a shape as the living room. Lexine's dried herbs still hung from her drying rack, up above the sink. A few plates were smashed—the ones probably on the counter—the shards in that same spiral pattern. The clean dishes still sat stacked up in the cupboards. Even the knives in the old butcher block looked untouched.

The only thing Franklin found amiss was that the jar of bacon grease, that Lexine always kept next to the stove, was empty.

Some ghost had licked it clean.

FRANKLIN WENT BACK OUT to the living room, looking for a blanket to cover up Lexine. She looked indecent like that.

No wonder Mama had looked sad when Franklin had mentioned Lexine's name.

Mama had known Lexine was already dead.

Although Franklin could only really see spirits when he was with Lexine, and Lexine was now dead, he still felt like something else was there—maybe the soul of her cabin. It didn't feel malicious or evil, not the same as what had done this.

"I'm afraid she's gone," Franklin said addressing whatever was there. "I'm sorry." He paused, then added, "I'm gonna find them and stop them." He didn't know about punishing a spirit or a ghost. If he knew how to send this one to Hell he sure would.

Before Franklin could drag a blanket over Lexine, he heard sirens wailing.

Had Charlene tried calling him? To tell him the police were coming or had a clue?

He wouldn't find out until he got back in cell phone range again. But he wasn't about to stick around and find out why the police were on their way. Sheriff Thompson was a good man, but he didn't have much imagination. Franklin being here would cause all kinds of heartache.

As Franklin turned to leave, a chill raced up his spine. He held himself ready to fly out of there if it was some spirit he'd never met before.

But it was Gloria. And she was carrying something. It looked like a black ball of hate, until she dropped it.

An ear of corn rolled next to a pool of Lexine's blood.

The ear of corn from Karl's fields.

That had Franklin's fingerprints on it.

How the hell had Gloria done that? Most ghosts didn't have the strength to carry something as heavy as an ear of corn, let alone for miles and miles.

When Franklin made to pick it up, Gloria barred her teeth at him and stood in his way.

Damn it!

Franklin had to get out of there. He did *not* want to be there with the cops coming.

It would take them a while to lift any prints off the corn, if they could get any at all. Plus, Franklin wasn't in the system: Mama had made damn sure he'd kept his nose clean, and for once, was grateful for her interfering ways.

Franklin ran out of the house and hauled his bike around back, to the trails there. He knew another way out of the woods that Lexine had shown him. Bushes scratched his legs as he ran, and got tangled in the wire wheels. The heat felt like a weight, heavy and trying to slow him down. The sirens kept getting close. Franklin knew he was out of sight of the cabin but he kept running, as if that thing that had killed his cousin was coming after him.

When Franklin finally got back to the main road, Gloria stood there, waiting for him in the hot sun.

"Why the hell did you do that?" Franklin yelled, madder than a hornet. "Sending me to jail won't make me a criminal. I'm never stealing Karl's crop of corn! You hear me?" Karl was his competition. Winning through cheating wasn't winning at all.

Gloria's glare didn't change, and she didn't look one bit guilty.

Franklin took a look at his legs. If Mama had been alive, she'd have thrown a fit over how bloody and scratched up he was. His shirt was ruined too. After tearing out another branch and a few more leaves from his wheels, Franklin got on his bike and started riding wearily back into town.

Why had Gloria dropped that ear of corn there? People didn't always make sense, and ghosts, even less so.

Or maybe—because it *was* an ear of corn from Karl's fields, they'd go see him.

Why would Gloria want the cops to go see Karl?

Franklin shook his head. He needed to get home, get cleaned up, maybe do some chores, but then he was gonna have to pay Karl Metzger, his main competition, a visit.

THE DAY STAYED hot and muggy. Franklin tried to talk himself out of going to Karl's house, but he kept remembering Lexine's body, laying broken like one of Adrianna's art dolls. So he hauled out his bike and made the long trip from his property, up to the four-lane highway, through town and to the other side, where highway sixty-two split off. Franklin huffed as he rode up the hill, past Karl's fields, then up the steep driveway.

Karl's house was a tall, two-story old building, with gray half-circles covering the walls and white curly bits under the eaves and between the rails on the front porch. It had tall windows that reflected back the sunlight, not letting any inside. Graceful cherry trees stood on either side of the big wooden door, and neatly trimmed bushes ran along the edges. The Kentucky bluegrass that made up the lawn was thick and healthy, without a single brown spot.

An old black Chevy sat in the driveway, but no one was home when Franklin knocked on the door. When Franklin thought about it, he realized Karl was probably at the vegetable stand out on the highway: Franklin had probably ridden right by him. Damn it!

Franklin stomped back to his bike, then paused, looking out over Karl's fields. In front of the rows and rows of corn Karl had a healthy patch of tomatoes, with plump beauties bursting off the vines. Another patch held squash and cucumbers, the prickly leaves hiding more prizes, Franklin was sure. Along the side ran Karl's rows of walnut trees, that would fruit come fall.

Everything that Franklin touched grew, and grew well.

But all of Karl's crops grew with abundance.

It just wasn't fair. Franklin had good land, and he tended his fields with love. Why was every growing thing on Karl's land so much bigger and better?

It was like he was back in high school, when nothing he did was good enough no matter how hard he'd studied, he just could never get the gist of algebra or geometry, was always failing while everything came easy to Karl: He got the grades, the praise, and the girls.

Franklin got back on his bike and rode through town. As had been his luck that entire day, Karl had already closed the stand and gone home by the time Franklin reached it.

With a dejected sigh, Franklin rode the rest of the way back to his house. He was never gonna catch up to his competition, never gonna catch a break, was always gonna be stacking other people's produce. That was just his life.

FRANKLIN SPENT the rest of the night fixing the fence out front, replacing the light bulb that had burned out on the front porch, and cleaning out the yellowjackets who'd thought they'd found a home under the back eves. Anything to keep himself busy and not thinking about Lexine.

Mama didn't seem to have an opinion one way or the other about Karl, Gloria, or Lexine. She sat staring at the table—maybe sad? Maybe scared? She didn't seem as angry as she had been, though.

Franklin woke when it was still dark, a blaring noise startling him. It took him a moment to realize it was his phone ringing. According to his alarm, it was 4:17 AM.

He didn't recognize the name on the caller ID. Maybe some drunk, or maybe his cousin Darryl, in trouble again. "Hello?" Franklin said.

"You gotta get over here," Ray said urgently. "There's something attacking Adrianna. It's spinning around, throwing things and I can't even see it! It's like some kind of invisible whirlwind!"

"Shit," Franklin said, levering himself out of bed. It had to be the same thing that had attacked Lexine. Whatever had killed her had left behind those spiral patterns of torn paper and glass. "That thing's deadly, Ray."

"How do I stop it?" Ray demanded. "It's twirling, snatching things up, throwing them. And—"

"I'm coming over as fast as I can get there," Franklin said as he shoved one leg, then the other, into his jeans, wincing as the cloth scratched over his cuts from that afternoon.

How could Ray defend himself and Adrianna against that thing? What did it want? Why was it attacking her? Why had it gone after Lexine and the businessman?

"Get Adrianna outside," Franklin added. He didn't know if it'd be safer there, but Adrianna, like Lexine, was only inside a place because they had to be: The rest of the time, they lived outdoors. Adrianna was a free spirit, and lived better in the open air.

"Good," Ray said. "Now get here." Then he hung up.

Franklin rushed out of the house, not bothering to turn on any lights. Mama had her own kind of special glow from her seat at the kitchen table. She didn't even raise her head as Franklin passed.

Something was bothering Mama. Franklin didn't have a clue what. But he couldn't stop and ask.

Cool night air blew against Franklin's face as he raced down the lane, then the street, and to the highway. This was one time he wished he had a car. But wishes weren't fishes. The far off horizon was starting to pink up. Franklin pushed himself to pedal faster, staying in the street instead of switching to the sidewalk when the four-lane narrowed down. None of the homes Franklin passed had on any lights. It was like one of those towns in a horror movie, with him as the sole survivor.

Franklin put that thought out of his head. He needed to think about what would help Adrianna. The thing liked lard and bacon grease. Shit. He should have brought another jar of Sweet Bess' lard with him, to try to draw it off. Maybe Adrianna had something like that in the kitchen. Or maybe just salt would do it—most ghosts liked things that were salty.

At the Sorrels', Franklin threw his bike against the fence and pounded on the gate. Ray opened it in short order, dressed in a white undershirt, brightly checked shorts and flip flops, his hair all messed. He nodded grimly to Franklin and held the gate open for him.

Franklin raced inside. The friendly mess of the statues and found art had been replaced by the chaos of decimation. All the daisies and pinwheels had been flattened. The hubcap man lay on the ground, broken in two. Just wisps of the colorful streamers remained, their long tails shredded.

"What would do such a thing?" Ray asked as they hurried down the path to where Adrianna sat, underneath her men wired together out of fallen tree branches. She wore a nightgown, like what a child might wear, white with pink flowers on it, a high collar, and long sleeves.

Franklin pulled up right quick when he realized the tree men hadn't been damaged. In fact, if anything, they seemed taller, bigger. They bent over, protectively, above Adrianna. She, in return, held one of their branches, like lovers holding hands, looking up at it, her face shining.

The trees weren't full of ghosts, that much Franklin could say. They weren't spirits, either, as far as he could tell. They were something different, maybe unique to Adrianna, and how she'd made 'em come alive.

"Miss Adrianna?" Franklin asked quietly.

When Adrianna looked at him, he saw two long gouges running down her left cheek, still bleeding. "Thank you, Franklin," she said, letting go of the tree man's hand and standing up.

Was it just the bad light, or did the hand fall in slow motion, as if unwilling to let go?

"I didn't do nothing," Franklin said. "I just got here. Looks like you did something, though, to drive it away."

"Wasn't me," Adrianna said, beaming and reaching back to pet one of the tree men. "They took care of us. Wouldn't let that thing come near me."

"But you were the one who told us to get outside," Ray said. He patted Franklin's back. "Thank you. Now, tell me, *what the hell was that thing?*"

Franklin took a step back from Ray's anger. "I don't rightly know," he said, shrugging. It was the truth. He really didn't know what this thing was.

All he knew was that it had to be stopped.

When Franklin turned to Adrianna, she shrugged as well, before she said, "It's a spirit. Jealous."

"And greedy," Franklin added. "It's been after my special lard." At least, he thought it was the same thing. Only something mighty strong could take off the lid of the jar of lard, as well as do the destruction he saw here.

"Why did it attack Adrianna?" Ray asked. He held out his hand to her.

Franklin was relieved to see how easy she took it and went into his arms. He'd been worried that since Ray hadn't saved her, she might no longer treasure him like she should.

"I don't know why it attacked Miss Adrianna," Franklin said. He turned to her. "You said it was jealous? Of what?"

"It wanted my eyes," Adrianna said. She shivered and turned her face into Ray's shoulder. "It wanted to see like I do."

"How do you see, Miss Adrianna?" Franklin asked quietly. "What do you see?" She'd never really talked about seeing before. Any more than he'd talked about his ghosts.

"The lines of power, of course," Adrianna said. She gestured to the ground, to the path she'd made Ray move, then to the tree men, then to the pond. "Can't you see them?"

A ghostly image of long white streams wavered above the places Adrianna pointed to. The image collapsed quickly, but not before Franklin realized that each stream connected to the other, and the places where they joined were stronger, not weaker, as the streams flowed together.

"No, ma'am, I can't," Franklin said. "Not clear, like you. Ray? Can you see what Adrianna's talking about?"

"No," Ray replied, then he bent his head down and kissed Adrianna's curls. "You were always special," he said fondly.

Was that why the spirit attacked Adrianna? Because she had some kind of power? Franklin hadn't known she was like him.

Who else in town was like that? Was there anyone else? Or was the spirit going to attack Franklin next? And if it did, where would he be safe? In his corn field, maybe? What would protect him?

"Will it come back?" Ray asked.

Adrianna gave a merry laugh. "No, I don't think so. We drove it off, didn't we boys?" she said, addressing the tree men.

"Did you...hurt it?" Franklin asked, skeptical. He'd never seen anything that could actually hurt a spirit.

"Skewered it good, at least once," Adrianna said proudly.

Would an injured spirit return? Or seek an easier target?

The spirits around Lexine were usually hurt, and always returning to her for comfort.

"It might come back," Franklin warned. "I'd camp out here, for a day or so, at least."

"Camping!" Adrianna said, clapping her hands together. "We haven't been camping for ages."

"Then we should camp right here, under the trees," Ray said, encasing her hands in his and drawing them up to kiss them, quickly. "I'll get the tent. You stay here." He glanced at Franklin, who nodded: Yes, he'd stay here with Miss Adrianna while Ray cleaned up, got everything ready.

Not that Franklin felt he could do any good against this angry spirit.

CHAPTER 4

FRANKLIN THOUGHT ABOUT CALLING CHARLENE
and asking to take the day off, but it was Saturday, one of the busiest
days at the Kroger. So he promised the Sorrels he'd stop by again after
work, then rode his bike home as fast as he could. Maybe he wouldn't
be too late to work after he got into his uniform.

Besides, he didn't want to change anything in his routine, in case
the cops finally came to see him about his cousin.

Franklin had been expecting a call from Aunt Jasmine about
Lexine, but he hadn't heard anything yet. She must know by now,
right? Though Franklin and Lexine hadn't been close, they'd still been
cousins. And he was close enough with the rest of his family, seeing
them every Sunday at church, then going over to Aunt Jasmine's place
for Sunday dinner.

Franklin slowed as he approached the farm. A brown sheriff's
Crown Vic sat in the driveway. Sheriff Thompson leaned against
the door.

Shit.

Franklin didn't even know what he could tell the sheriff about the
Sorrels. He couldn't tell him that they'd been attacked by an angry
spirit—not without being hauled off for being crazy.

But the sheriff already knew something was going on. Nothing to it but for Franklin to tell as much of the truth as he could.

"Morning, Sheriff," Franklin said as he rode his bike into the driveway. "What can I do you for?" He casually got off his bike and walked up, telling himself again and again, *Nothing's wrong. Everything here's cool.*

"Where you been?" the sheriff asked as he pushed himself off the car and tipped his hat up a bit, showing his white face, tiny suspicious eyes, big nose, and disapproving grimace. The only thing soft about him was the big brown mustache he grew. He combed it frequently, lining all the hairs up neatly.

"Over at the Sorrels," Franklin admitted. "They was having a problem with their koi pond." While that might not be the first thing Ray would say when the sheriff asked about it, he would back Franklin up. Franklin had been there about the fish pond, if not that night.

"Didn't know you were also a speaker to the fish, not just a speaker to the dead." Sheriff Thompson grinned as if he'd made some kind of joke, though Franklin didn't get it.

Franklin just shrugged. He knew the reputation he—and the rest of his family—had in town. He wasn't surprised that the sheriff had heard the rumors.

"Anyway." The sheriff paused and looked down. "I'm here about your cousin Lexine."

"She in trouble?" Franklin asked. He'd prepared himself for that, as well as he could.

Those sharp eyes were back on his face again. Luckily, Franklin was already sweaty from his ride.

"You could say that. She's dead."

"What?" Franklin exclaimed. "No—what happened?" He kept easy eye contact, certain that those shows on TV weren't lying about everything. Eye contact meant he was telling the truth, that he was surprised.

"Murdered," Sheriff Thompson said. "I was sitting here, waiting for backup, in case you turned out to be the same."

"Murdered?" Franklin asked, unbelieving. "What? How? Who?"

"We'll find the bastards. Them and their wild animals. Really tore the place apart. You wouldn't happen to know of anyone who had a problem with Lexine?"

Franklin shook his head, as if bewildered. "I don't—I mean, there was that contractor. Who built her the house. And his wife. But they wouldn't do something like that." Franklin looked up. "I gotta go see Aunt Jasmine," he said. "I need to go see how she's doing."

The sheriff nodded and said, "I'm sorry for your loss."

"Thank you," Franklin said. He turned and walked his bike to the front porch. Guess he was calling Charlene, telling her he needed to take the day off.

"Say, you wouldn't happen to be missing any of your crop there, would you?" Sheriff Thompson asked casually.

"No sir, not that I know of," Franklin said, looking back over his shoulder, his heart pounding in his chest. "Why?"

"A few corn cobs were found around the bodies. Like some kind of ritual."

"Bodies?" Franklin asked, leaning his bike against the front porch and walking back toward the sheriff. "Did you say bodies? Who else was killed?" Franklin demanded.

"A businessman," the sheriff admitted. "Earl Jackson. Developer, come here to see about turning some of the nearby land into a resort. Did you know anything about that?"

"No, sir," Franklin said. "I can ask Aunt Jasmine about it, though."

"I've talked with her," the sheriff said with a sigh. "She didn't know anything either." He gave Franklin a softer look. "Give my regards to your aunt. And the rest of your family."

"I will. Thank you for letting me know, Sheriff," Franklin said. He paused, then asked, "You check with Karl Metzger? About his corn?"

"No. Why should I?" Sheriff Thompson asked.

Shit. Franklin shouldn't have said that. "Just a thought," he said as easily as he could. "You know. Since we're rivals and all. His family and mine. Coulda been his corn."

"You thinking he did this?" Sheriff Thompson said.

"No, no, not Karl," Franklin said, horrified. Had he just fallen into some kind of trap set by Gloria? Getting Karl in trouble because of the corn at the crime scene?

"I'll go talk with him. You take it easy," the sheriff said as he walked around his car and slid in.

Damn it. Franklin hadn't meant for the sheriff to start thinking Karl was a suspect. He also hadn't known that Gloria had carried more than one ear of corn to the cabin. She must have moved fast, as the sirens had been close.

However, there was nothing for Franklin to do but call work, shower, then gather with his family to mourn.

FRANKLIN SAT out on the back stoop with his older cousins: Darryl, Jason, and May. A slatted, yellow-painted wooden fence boxed in the yard, closing it off from the alley and its neighbors. A passel of younger kids ran around the browning grass. They didn't really understand what was going on, and they'd barely known Lexine. Since the adults had been so serious all day, they were now racing around like crazy things. Franklin couldn't really follow the rules of whatever game they were playing. It seemed like tag, only they were all bomber planes.

Darryl and May were drinking beer, of course, although Franklin suspected they might have spiked their cans with something more potent. Not because they was gonna miss Lexine that much— Franklin had been the closest to her—just any excuse to drink.

Jason sat quiet, alone with the three of them. He'd had to go with Aunt Jasmine to help identify the body, and he couldn't seem to shake what he'd seen.

Franklin couldn't either. How had a spirit broken her neck like that? And made those gouges? It was awfully strong, stronger than any spirit Franklin had ever heard about.

"You reckon you'll start seeing Lexine?" Darryl asked with a smirk as he took another drink. His blue work shirt had seen better days, and he used the sleeve to swipe at the sweat on his tall, shaved head. While Franklin's brown uniform shirt wasn't the best looking, at least he took care of it. Darryl's eyes was perpetually bloodshot, like he'd been in a smoky room, though his main indulgence was liquor. He had the same sharp nose as Aunt Jasmine, making his face look long and serious, though he was forever cracking jokes and laughing, usually at Franklin's expense.

"No," Franklin said. He'd be real surprised if she showed up to haunt him. She had power all on her own. She wouldn't need him to settle anything for her.

Except to find her killer.

"I still say it was a lover's spat," May said with a smile that wasn't appropriate and gave Franklin the willies. Mama would have *tsked* at how low cut her sundress was, though it was a pretty red. She'd straightened her hair again, and dyed part of it a lighter brown. She looked more like Mama and Franklin, with a rounder face, softer lips, and kinder brown eyes.

"No," Jason said firmly. "It weren't him. It weren't something human." He looked up finally and caught Franklin's eye. "Do you know what it was?"

Jason looked so tired. Was he coming down with something? Though he was the youngest, white still tinged the temples of his close-cropped brown 'fro. He was a meld of the two families, with a long nose, round face, and thin lips.

"Something evil," Franklin said.

May snorted. "Evil? Now you're sounding like Preacher Sinclair."

"None of your mouth, now," Jason said sternly. "Taking another life like that *is* evil. Nobody deserved that."

Franklin nodded. "It hasn't gone away, though," he warned.

"What, you think this thing's got a hard-on for our family?" Darryl asked. "If so, it can just say hello to my friends, misters Smith and Wesson."

Jason glared at Darryl. "That's the stupidest—"

"Rock salt," Franklin said.

Everyone looked at Franklin like he was nuts, a regard he was used to. "Shotgun, not filled with buckshot, but rock salt. That might help." The thing kept going after his lard, like a regular ghost would. And ghosts liked salty stuff. Maybe filling it with salt would distract it, or fill it so it would leave.

"I can do that," Darryl said, nodding slowly. "You need to borrow a gun?"

"Naw, got one," Franklin lied. He wouldn't ever borrow anything from Darryl. Never knew when Darryl might just show up on his doorstep, drunk, wanting to reclaim it.

"Why do you think it went after Lexine?" Jason asked, still trying to understand.

"'Cause she was special," Franklin said. He ignored May's snort. "That businessman, too. Earl Jackson. He must have had something. Otherwise it would have left him alone." He'd been trying to get away, and the thing had kept attacking him, while it had left Ray alone, and only gone after Adrianna.

"What kind of power did that fat old man have?" Darryl asked.

"I bet it wasn't his dick—men are the only ones who think they're magic," May said, laughing.

How much had May already had to drink? Franklin just shook his head.

"He was here to develop property, right? Maybe he could see the wealth flowing in," Jason said. "I'd love a power like that."

"Naw, maybe he found oil or gold or something, and wanted to dig it up," Darryl said, playing along for once.

Lexine had seen spirits. Franklin saw ghosts. Adrianna saw lines of power, which Franklin had always thought was some kind of mystic crap. Maybe the businessman could see money or future fame, though that didn't seem right—that was manmade, artificial, not natural from the earth.

"Someone at work said something about them making a resort here, right?" Franklin said, thinking out loud. "And maybe diverting the Wolf River."

"So maybe he was a dowser," Jason said.

"A what?" May asked.

Jason said, "Someone who can find water. They used to be real respected, could find the place where you should dig your well. Used a dowsing rod." At the collective blank looks, Jason added, "I read about it once."

"You were always the brainy one," Darryl said. "The brain, the weirdo, the slut, and the hick. Here's to the four of us," he added, raising his can in salute.

"Who you calling a slut? Asshole," May said, thwapping him on the arm.

"Sounds like the start of a bad joke," Franklin said. "What, do we all go into a bar or something?"

Darryl laughed. "Say, did you hear the one about—"

A wail rose from one of the kids—Jason's daughter—she'd run headlong into Darryl's son, and now had a bloody nose. While Jason and May went to go deal with them, Franklin sat in silence with Darryl, wondering.

Jason had always been attracted to water, had loved swimming more than any of them. He could find a path to a crick more easily than a water roach in a drought.

Had Jason been talking about himself? Did he have a power too?

What if that thing went after his cousin Jason next?

FRANKLIN TRIED to find a time to talk with Jason on his own, but then there was dinner, with people bringing over food, then getting the kids ready for bed, so Franklin didn't have a chance.

The coroner finally said she'd release the body by Wednesday, so they wouldn't be able to schedule the funeral until Thursday. It would be closed casket, something that made Aunt Jasmine howl and Jason and the others hurry her to her bed.

Franklin went home after that, glad to see Mama was back to her glaring self. Gloria was there as well, sitting side-by-side at the kitchen table like an old married couple. But Gloria was tapping her nails again, *click click click*.

Franklin didn't know what Gloria was waiting for, but it was something. Her impatience filled the kitchen, making his skin itch like ants was crawling all over it.

"What is it that thing wants?" Franklin asked as he settled in with a tall glass of sweet tea. The only light in the kitchen was from the stove, behind him. It didn't make the ghosts more human: In the gloom, they glowed with their own weird light.

"Why did it kill Lexine? Why did you bring those cobs of Karl's corn to the cabin? Were you trying to get him arrested?"

Neither of the ghosts replied. Franklin wished for one of Darryl's beers, or even a straight shot of bourbon. The night felt loose and dangerous. Was that creature going to come after him next? Or Jason? How could Franklin defend himself? Or his family? Or the other special people in town?

Franklin had more questions than answers. And the uncomfortable feeling that this was just the beginning.

FRANKLIN ARRANGED to work only half a day the next day, then only half a day on Thursday, the day of the funeral.

That morning, he put on his Sunday best—short-sleeved white shirt, blue tie, and dark blue suit—and went to church to be with his family. The building was modern, which made Franklin more comfortable: Fewer ghosts haunting the sanctuary. White stone went up to a tall arched roof, with plain glass in most of the windows, the fund-raiser to replace them with stained glass ongoing.

Miss Karen and Miss Kay stood outside, greeting everyone, a pair of spinster aunts who Franklin had thought were ancient when he'd been a boy over fifteen years ago.

"We're so sorry for your loss," they both said, holding his hand in their soft white gloves. They wore identical corsages on their bright lavender and yellow dresses, hats shading their dark faces from even the most slender beam of sunlight.

"You let us know if we can do anything to help," Miss Karen added.

"Anything at all," Miss Kay said, getting in the last word.

"We will," Franklin promised, though he didn't want to get anywhere near the sisters' constant feud to outdo each other.

After stepping across the threshold, Franklin paused to let his eyes adjust. Tables in the nave held huge vases filled with gladiolas and spiky ferns: Franklin knew he'd be seeing them again at the funeral. The red tile floor held in the cool from the AC. To the right were two darkened staircases, one going upstairs to the classrooms, the other downstairs to the kitchen and community hall.

Franklin considered going downstairs—they'd still be serving coffee and pastries—but he caught sight of Jason in the sanctuary so stepped in there instead.

Light-colored wooden beams lifted the peaked roof, as if raising it closer to God. Franklin liked the openness of the room, how the aisle running down the center was wide enough for three lines of folks. The cross at the front was carved out of dark wood, and the same dark wood made up the pulpit.

"Hey," Franklin said, sliding into the pew behind Jason.

Jason turned around. "Hey," he said, holding out his hand, giving Franklin a firm shake.

"Morning, Lisa, Karen," Franklin greeted Jason's two girls.

Jason's wife Elise wasn't there. She hadn't been at Aunt Jasmine's earlier, now that Franklin thought about it. Should he ask?

"Elise's still sick," Jason said before Franklin could mention it. "Horrible flu."

"I'm sorry to hear that. Is there anything I can bring her? Soup from the store?"

"Thanks," Jason said. "You could come over and babysit sometime."

Franklin gave a mock shudder. "For these two hellions?" he teased.

"Uncle Franklin," Lisa complained.

"We're not as bad as Tommy," Karen added—Darryl's youngest, the one who'd given her a bloody nose the day before.

"True," Franklin said. "I suppose I could come by some night.

Give you some relief from these two," he said. Then he paused. Would it be safe? Were any of his family safe around him while that thing was still out there, stalking them?

"It'll be fine," Jason said, interrupting Franklin's thoughts.

Franklin nodded, but he wasn't sure. Unfortunately, because the girls were there and without their mother, Franklin couldn't get Jason on his own.

Darryl, May, and Aunt Jasmine came in a short while later, with all their kids and spouses and friends. The family huddled together in misery in the front pews.

However, Franklin felt out of place. He didn't enjoy Preacher Sinclair's comments on how Lexine had found a better place—Lexine had been perfectly happy on her own. She'd stopped coming to church when she'd come of age. Hadn't stopped praying, just followed her own path.

Franklin did know Lexine had passed on, though he was never sure what that meant. Did the ghosts he helped go onto Heaven? He doubted they went to Hell—they weren't ever fearful. They needed help, not counseling.

Finally, the service was over. Franklin felt as impatient as Gloria, squeezing his hands together, waiting while the reception line passed by Preacher Sinclair.

It wasn't that the preacher was a bad person. He just had a different view of the world than Franklin, who'd help every soul who asked him, not just those who was saved.

After they'd finally passed that gauntlet, Franklin went over to Jason. His girls were playing with their other cousins, and Franklin finally got a chance to speak to Jason alone.

"You remember what you were saying about dowsers?" Franklin asked, standing with his arms crossed, watching the girls instead of his cousin.

"Yeah," Jason said warily.

"You wasn't describing yourself, were you?" Franklin asked.

"Why would you ask that?" Jason said. "I ain't like you."

"You sure?" Franklin asked, finally turning and looking at Jason. "This thing attacked the Sorrels too. Adrianna."

Jason gave a dark chuckle. "Of course, *she's* gonna be special like you. But it ain't me you should be giving warnings to. I'm just a plain Joe. Nothing special about me."

Why was Jason so bitter? Did it have something to do with Elise's "illness"?

"If you're not the one I should be talking to, who is?" Franklin asked.

"You won't believe me," Jason said.

"Try me."

"Darryl."

Franklin opened his mouth, then shut it again. "You're right. I don't believe you." Of all his older cousins, Darryl had always been the hardest on Franklin when they'd been growing up, always teasing him about seeing things that weren't there, calling him crazy and freak and weirdo.

"It's easiest to hate yourself, hate your own kind," Jason said.

Franklin couldn't help his laugh. "You read that in a book somewhere too?"

"Sure," Jason said easily.

"What's going on?" Franklin asked, concerned.

"Nothing."

"Really?"

"Elsie's been sick a lot," Jason said quietly. "I've been dealing with the girls on my own too much." He gave a false smile. "Come by Wednesday night. If you dare."

Franklin let Jason go, though he was still worried.

But he couldn't help someone—human or ghost—who didn't want help, or wouldn't ask for what they needed.

FRANKLIN KNEW BETTER than to accuse Darryl of being special, or even asking him directly. Darryl might say something when he was drunk. Then again, he was drunk so often, he could probably control himself, at least a hell of a lot better than Franklin could, who rarely drank.

So how could Franklin get Darryl to talk with him? Or to take his warning seriously? Franklin couldn't figure out a plan as he stacked carrots, or mopped up spilled milk, or even as he rode his bike home. He'd had to stay late that night at the Kroger, so he'd go and see the Sorrels the next night.

As Franklin rode up to his house, he saw Darryl's pickup in the driveway of his farm.

Maybe he wouldn't have to come up with something to say.

Darryl sat on Franklin's front porch, only four of a six-pack of beer still unopened sitting next to him.

"Jason told me he'd been blabbing his big mouth," Darryl said as Franklin walked up.

"Maybe," Franklin said, sitting down carefully next to Darryl on the steps. Darryl could be mean as a cornered snake and sometimes settled things with his fists. "You wanna tell me what's going on?"

"No," Darryl said. He took another long slug of beer and looked out at his truck.

"Then why the hell you here?" Franklin said as the silence continued.

"You really think that thing came after Lexine because she was special?" Darryl asked after another long pause.

"Yeah, that's what makes sense," Franklin said. "But I don't know for sure. Can't figure out what it wants. Besides my good lard."

"I don't see stuff like you and Lexine," Darryl said finally.

"Then you ain't got nothing to worry about, do you?" Franklin said. He was tired and hungry and wished Darryl would just get on with it or leave.

"But sometimes, like when I'm hunting, I get a feeling, you know? Like I can see the trail of an animal. It's like a clear path through the bush."

"Maybe you're just seeing the clues that most folks miss," Franklin said, trying to help Darryl out.

"Exactly! Like if a branch is bent, or if there's spoor or a hoof print. That kind of thing."

"So you ain't special," Franklin clarified. "You're just a good hunter."

"Right." Darryl took another long gulp of beer. "Just that—I see those things whether they're there or not. That trail." He finished his beer, crushed the can, threw it out into the driveway, then opened the next.

Franklin knew better than to say something about not making a mess. He'd just be called a Suzie Homemaker again, or worse.

"I can always see where an animal's been. Whether it's daylight or dark. Whether there's really a trail left behind by a critter or not." Darryl sighed and looked at his beer can.

"So you see animal trails through the woods. That no one else can see. Right? For all kinds of animals? Or just the ones you're hunting?" Franklin asked. What kind of thing was Darryl seeing?

"I gotta be hunting it. And serious, too. If I'm just farting around out there, nothing shows up." Darryl said, finally warming up to his subject. "It's why I switched to bow hunting, two seasons back. It felt like too much of an unfair advantage, you know? I wasn't having to sit in a blind like those other guys. I could always just find a trail. Go after my deer."

"When'd you start seeing your trails?" Franklin asked, curious.

"Fourteen, fifteen. Something like that. I think I might've been seeing 'em before, too, but I didn't know what I was seeing. I just thought I was a good tracker, you know?"

"Right when your dad left?" Franklin asked. Then he pressed his lips together, wishing he could take the words back. His step-uncle had left Aunt Jasmine with four kids, a stack of bills, and angry creditors, calling at all hours.

Lexine had never talked much about her dad after that. Franklin wondered sometimes if she'd found a way to get revenge on him, 'cause she did mention once that his dreams were never gonna be sweet, not 'til he died.

"Yeah." Darryl said shortly. "Just before he left, I showed him, how I could see." He sighed and took another drink. "Was I the reason he left? Hell if I know. He hated Lexine. Hated how she was different. Was happy to drop her off in exchange for 'his boys.' But I never trusted him, not like Jason."

"I thought you two were like lost souls who'd finally found each other," Franklin said, stunned. Their biological dad had left right after Jason, the youngest, had been born. Franklin remembered how happy Darryl and Jason had been with their new Dad, following him around and always imitating him. He'd never liked Franklin, either, which was part of why Darryl had always been so hard on him.

"Sure, it was like that for a while. I mean, it was nice to have a man in the home, you know?" Darryl said. "Or maybe you don't. Your mama never picked up with anyone, did she."

"Mama always said she'd lost her one true love in the war," Franklin said. He'd never known Mama to date, even. He'd wondered, once he was in his twenties, if she'd start going out. She'd started dressing nicer, and maybe...but then she'd never taken care of herself, and wouldn't go see a doctor even when the chest pains started.

"But Dad, well, he wasn't one for seeing what was there, you know?" Darryl said. "He'd say that things were fine when they weren't, or that we had money when we didn't. It was like he kept thinking that saying a thing would make it true. It never did."

"When'd you get to be so smart?" Franklin asked, amazed at his cousin.

Darryl grinned at Franklin. "Had it beat into me by the school of hard knocks."

"Didn't know they could get anything through that wooden block sitting on top of your shoulders," Franklin teased back.

They sat on the stoop in the cooling night, the crickets bringing up their chorus.

"So, you want to go out hunting?" Darryl finally asked.

"No," Franklin said, confused. "I don't really hunt." After Lexine had shown him how the spirit of an animal stayed near its body when it'd been wounded, not killed outright, he hadn't had the heart.

"No, idiot. I mean *hunting*. Like tracking this thing that killed Lexine."

"Oh!" Franklin said.

"I figure it's an animal-like thing, right? So let's go out into the woods, behind Lexine's cabin. Let's see if I can't track this thing."

For the first time in a week, Franklin had hope. "And I'll bring some of my special lard. As bait."

"See, Cuz? I knew you weren't completely useless. Just mostly."

"Same to you," Franklin replied.

CHAPTER 5

FRANKLIN WAS GLAD THAT CHARLENE was understanding about family when he went in to ask her about taking more time off.

The command center screens showed the produce section, the two checkout lanes, the beer and wine cooler, and the outside of the store. Charlene wore her usual uniform, sitting with her feet on a small stool, flicking through the displays.

"Hey, honey," Charlene said. "How you holding up?"

"I'm okay," Franklin said. "But Aunt Jasmine asked us to come over this afternoon. Evidently there's a will, and we all need to be there when it's read." Which was sort of the truth. There was a will, and they were gathering that night at dinner to read it.

"I understand," Charlene said, nodding. She put her feet on the floor and turned to face him. "You go be with your family this afternoon."

"Thanks, Charlene. You're the best," Franklin said.

"You doing okay?" Charlene asked, the warmth in her voice coming through loud and clear. "You look tired."

Franklin nodded, not sure what else to say. Darryl had stayed way too late, making Franklin miss his Ab-Buster workout as well as snooze his alarm twice that morning.

"Losing Lexine like that. Quite a shock. You go ahead and take the rest of the day off. Tomorrow, too, if you need it. Just call."

"Thanks, Charlene," Franklin said, relieved. "You're the best. I'll work double shifts next week, or volunteer for the whole time we're doing inventory."

Charlene chuckled. "I may just hold you to that. Now, take care of yourself. Go be with your family."

"I'll tell 'em you were asking about them," Franklin said as he left. He only felt a little guilty for taking the afternoon off—he was going to be spending time with his family.

Darryl counted as family, right?

Franklin rode home, changed out of his uniform, picked up another jar of lard, then rode out to Lexine's.

Sun blazed down on the blacktop road. The air was sticky and wet, and smelled like hot tar. Even the shade under the trees brought little relief, though at least it smelled more like pine there. Franklin was soaked through by the time he rode up the path to Lexine's cabin.

Darryl's big black truck was already there, parked a bit down the road. Yellow police tape—just like what Franklin had seen on TV—was strung across the road, blocking the driveway. The businessman's SUV no longer sat parked there.

The door to Lexine's cabin had more police tape over it in an X. The police had passed along the name of a company who would come out and clean the cabin once they released it. Right now, it was still a crime scene.

Sweet Bess showed up as Franklin got off his bike. *Shit.* Darryl might be a bit more friendly right now, but he'd tease Franklin mercilessly if he ran away from a spirit.

The big sow glared at Franklin and pawed at the ground. Oh hell. Was it even angrier because Franklin had some of her lard on him?

A crashing noise came from the side. Darryl came out of the trees, wearing dark jeans and a bright orange T-shirt.

Darryl looked at Franklin, then at the spot Franklin stared at. "You got that crazy look on you. What the hell are you seeing?"

"A sow. One I slaughtered this spring. Sweet Bess." Franklin edged closer to Darryl, as if that might stop the sow from ramming him.

"That monster? I remember her." Darryl said. He gave a low whistle. "So what can she do to you?"

"She's run at me before," Franklin admitted. "And when a spirit or a ghost goes through you—" He stopped and shuddered. It'd take him at least a day to recover.

"How about I go through it?" Darryl said. He walked forward, straight through Sweet Bess.

The spirit disappeared.

"Did you feel anything? Franklin asked, surprised.

Darryl gave a quick shake of his shoulders. "Naw, not really. Just —like I was passing through an extra shadow, you know?"

"Thank you," Franklin said, leaning his bike against Darryl's truck. It should be safe there.

"How bad is it, do you think?" Darryl asked, pointing toward the cabin with his chin.

"Pretty bad," Franklin said. He wasn't about to admit he'd already seen it.

"Let's go," Darryl said, striding off toward the cabin.

Franklin followed, also curious. They ducked under the yellow tape across the driveway and approached the cabin, which sat still and empty. The front window was still dark, and now, from outside, Franklin heard the flies buzzing.

Darryl paused and put his hands up against the glass to see better. "Jesus," he muttered.

Franklin walked around the side of the cabin, to see in through the blown-out window. The cops hadn't covered it up, and it framed the scene with fragments of broken glass around the edges.

The police had moved the couch, probably to get a stretcher in, for the bodies. Blood lay dark and heavy on the floor. None of the cobs of corn remained—Franklin figured they'd been taken into evidence. Paper and glass still lay strewn in a spiral pattern.

"That's just messed up," Darryl said, coming to stand beside Franklin. "You think she fought back?"

"With everything she had," Franklin said. But it was hard to fight something you couldn't see.

"Let's get this bastard," Darryl said grimly. He turned and headed back to the truck.

"We'll find whatever did this," Franklin promised. Though that was also his fear.

~

DARRYL HAULED a backpack from the bed of his black pickup truck. "Here," he said, thrusting it at Franklin.

The weight of the bag surprised Franklin. "What the hell you got in this thing?"

"Extra ammo, water, energy bars, emergency kit, like that." Darryl hauled out a second backpack that was similarly packed. From under the seats of the front cabin, he pulled out two shotguns. "Have you shot one of these before?" Darryl asked.

Franklin held it up and looked it over. "They're like the ones we used when we went hunting with your dad." The shotgun had the safety on and it wasn't loaded.

"These are probably the exact same ones we used as kids," Darryl said proudly. "They're all clean, oiled, and in good working condition."

Franklin felt better that Darryl took care of his guns, took them seriously. And also, that there wasn't any beer or bourbon in his pack.

"Did you see a trail of the thing in Lexine's cabin?" Franklin asked as they finished getting themselves ready.

Darryl shook his head. "Don't mean nothing, though. Needed to get ready. As I said, just farting around don't cut it. Got to be hunting before any kind of trail shows up."

"Where do you want to start?" Franklin asked.

"Think that thing came in the front? Or the back?" Darryl asked in return.

Franklin thought for a moment. "I bet it came in the front, then went out the back." Because it had probably attacked Lexine first, which gave the businessman time to run away.

"The businessman was in the kitchen, wasn't he? You think he was attacked second?" Darryl said as they walked back toward the cabin again.

"Yeah," Franklin said. He couldn't mention the bloody door, how the businessman had been trying to get out. At least the businessman's ghost had passed on, or was haunting someone else if it hadn't.

The trees loomed a few feet from the house, as if they were just waiting to take the land back. Leaves and scraggly grass covered the dirt path going from the front to the back. The chorus of cicadas was deafening, cycling up and down, like sirens.

Darryl walked right up to the first kitchen window, Franklin beside him. They couldn't see much—the thing hadn't been as destructive there, and the counter hid the floor where the body had been.

"See anything?" Franklin asked. All he received was a glare.

Darryl looked through the window above the sink, then the one over the kitchen table, but he didn't seem to find anything.

"What are you looking for?" Franklin asked, still curious.

"A way to shut your hole," Darryl complained. He glared at Franklin, who grinned at him. "This was what it was like, wasn't it, when we found out about your gift? Us asking about it all the time?"

"Maybe," Franklin said, rocking back on his heels, delighted. "You know what they say about payback."

"That he's a bitch about to get his ass kicked? Yeah, I heard that," Darryl said, sounding mean.

Franklin didn't care. It still felt good to get back at Darryl for all those years of teasing.

Out behind Lexine's house, the trees had been cut back further, giving Lexine a place for a garden. Franklin was going to have to come out and tend it once a week or so, until they'd settled what they was gonna do with her place. Tall okra plants grew along one side, standing like prickly guards. Lexine's purple and red heirloom tomatoes needed harvesting. The yellow and green striped squashes were nearly ripe as well. Franklin didn't know what to do with all her herbs—sage, oregano, rosemary, thyme, basil, and others. Maybe he could dry 'em out, like Lexine had, and sell 'em in town.

Darryl scouted from the cabin to Lexine's garden, then back again, then out, walking in wider circles, always examining the earth, looking for some footprint or clue or the hint of a trail. He reminded Franklin of a hound trying to catch a scent.

At the edge of the woods, where the path started, Darryl called Franklin over. "Something came through here recently. It was big, moving fast. See this broken twig?"

Franklin winced. That damage had probably been caused by him, leaving with his bike. "Ghosts don't generally go through things, or along paths. They just disappear and reappear."

"Something went this way. Come on. It's as good a place to start as any."

"You know this path leads back to the main road, right?" Franklin called after Darryl as he hurried along, the bushes slapping at his legs. At least this time Franklin was better prepared, wearing thick jeans and boots.

"Yeah," Darryl said, unerringly turning where Franklin had turned, taking the same trail. "So maybe it isn't some kind of spirit we're hunting. Maybe it had some human help."

"Okay," Franklin said, though he knew it wasn't the case. If anything, the spirit had had ghostly help, from Gloria.

Were Gloria and the spirit connected? If so, what connected them? How were they connected? They'd both shown up at about the same time. . . .

Darryl stopped just before they took the final left to the highway. Sunlight filtered down through the pines above them. The air felt still and thick. He swung his head to the right and the left, his back hunched, like a left guard about to make a flying tackle. He held up his hand and kept looking around, his eyes growing unfocused, his mouth slack.

Was that what Franklin looked like? When he talked with a ghost? Darryl didn't seem to be all there anymore.

No wonder people thought Franklin was crazy if he looked that way.

Suddenly, Darryl took off again through the woods, going a different direction. They weren't following no proper path—it was more like a deer trail.

Franklin hadn't ever gone this way before, though he was sure Lexine had. She'd know every inch of land surrounding hers, and probably all the property marked private as well.

Branches grew across the path that Darryl leaped over with ease. He slid to the left or right, avoiding brambles gracefully. Not a leaf stirred as he ran and his footsteps were silent.

Franklin had never seen his cousin move that way. Had Darryl's sight lent the hick a grace he'd never had before?

Squirrels chittered at them from above. Some small creature—a rabbit, probably—bounded away through the dry leaves of the underbrush as they came up. The cicadas kept up their deafening cries. Franklin felt a headache creeping up from the back of his skull.

Darryl paused at the edge of a clearing. It was barely fifteen feet across, just a pause in the trees.

Franklin looked out and felt his heart push hard against his chest.

What the fuck was that?

On the far side of the clearing hung a gray dust devil. It was maybe three feet tall, and another couple wide. It could have been a tumbleweed, but it had black vines growing through it, laced with sharp thorns. It floated two feet off the ground, whirling in place.

Even from where they stood, Franklin felt it radiating *evil*. Its *intent* was clear: It hated him and all those like him, viewed them as competitors and prey. It planned on getting rid of all of them, dipping its thorns into their flesh, ripping out what made them special.

"Shit," Darryl said. "We got to help him."

"What? Are you crazy?" Franklin said, reaching out and grabbing Darryl's arm. That thing didn't need their help.

Without warning, the thing whirled toward them, arms failing, intent on cutting them to ribbons. Franklin tried holding Darryl back but his stubborn cousin shook him off and walked into the clearing.

The thing disappeared before Darryl reached the other edge.

Only then did Franklin see the man on the ground.

～

"HEY, MISTER, YOU OKAY?" Darryl asked as he knelt down.

The man lay just under the edge of the trees. The cicadas cycled up loudly, filling the air with their screeching. Smells of mulching leaves and black dirt floated up.

"Is he breathing?" Franklin asked as he came up.

"Yeah, he's still alive," Darryl said.

Franklin looked over Darryl's shoulder. The man was white, mid-fifties he'd guess, and probably some kind of bum, given how beat up and dirty his clothes were, how the dirt was caked along the wrinkles of his face, and how blistered up and sunburnt his hands were. He had gouges in his right cheek where the thing had attacked him, the same gouges that Franklin had seen in the businessman's face, and the two long scars running down Adrianna's cheek.

"Water," Darryl snapped at Franklin.

Franklin shrugged off his backpack and handed over his extra bottle. The man looked in bad shape.

"What do you think he was doing here?" Darryl asked.

"He was being attacked," Franklin said quietly. "See the gouges on his face?"

"That thing? Was it here?" Darryl asked as he wet a kerchief and washed the man's face.

"Yeah. It was standing right over him," Franklin said. He shivered. He had no idea what the hell that creature was. It wasn't natural, though. It wasn't a regular spirit. Why could he see it? Normally, he only saw ghosts.

"Why didn't you shoot it?" Darryl demanded.

"I—I—it don't matter. You'll be able to track it again," Franklin protested. "Besides, there was this guy here."

"All right," Darryl said with a sigh. He turned back to the bum. "Come on, buddy, there you go." He raised the man up a little and tried giving him a drink of water.

The man sputtered and coughed, then heaved a huge sigh before he opened his eyes. At the sight of the pair of them, he suddenly sat up and scrambled backwards, trying to get away.

"Hey, hey!" Darryl said, reaching out and grabbing the guy's leg so he couldn't get away. "We ain't here to hurt you."

The man reached up and touched his cheek gingerly. "Yeah?" he said, disbelieving.

"We didn't do that," Franklin assured him. "Look, I'm Franklin, this here's my cousin Darryl."

"Billy," the man said. He looked fearfully beyond them out into the clearing. "You sure it wasn't some kind of dog or trained wild animal? Something that's with you two?" His voice sounded like sandpaper roughed over hard stones.

Franklin didn't bother pointing out that an animal that was wild was the opposite of trained.

"It wasn't us," Darryl said. "Or any animal we have with us. It's— wild. We was tracking it."

Billy nodded. "I ain't never seen anything like it before. That doesn't mean it wasn't some kind of trick that you two pulled."

Darryl rolled his eyes, but Franklin asked, "What did you see?"

"Some kind of whirling light. Calling to me, out here, under the trees," Billy said. "Haven't been hitting the hooch today," he added defensively. Then he paused. "Okay, only a bit, though. So I followed it. Then it attacked me." He looked suspiciously at Franklin and Darryl again.

"We came up while it was standing over you. You were down on the ground," Franklin said. "We chased it off."

"You still should have shot it," Darryl complained.

Billy shook his head. "Won't catch that thing with guns."

"What do you mean?" Franklin asked. "What do you think it was?"

"Evil," Billy countered. He looked straight at Franklin, his watery brown eyes suddenly sharp and clear. "And the only thing that'll combat that thing is love."

Darryl scoffed. "Right. We're supposed to hug it to death. No, we got good rock salt here, ready to blast it to bits."

"Do you think that'll work?" Billy asked Franklin, ignoring Darryl.

"It likes salty things," Franklin replied. He really didn't know what else to do.

"Right, which is why it was licking my cheek," Billy said sarcastically. "That thing's a killer. And it'll come back after me, won't it?"

Franklin hesitated, but he had to tell Billy the truth. "Yeah, it might. But I ain't never seen anything like it before, so I don't know for certain."

"Okay. Guess I better go break the law, then," Billy said as he heaved himself up.

Franklin and Darryl stood as well. "What do you mean?" Franklin asked.

"He breaks the law, he'll be thrown in jail for the night, maybe two. You think a few bars are gonna stop that thing?" Darryl asked.

"Nope," Billy replied. "But being around a bunch of other folks will. It drew me out here, away from the others. Now, they're a sorry group. I wouldn't trust 'em with my sister, and she's both a black belt and a whore. They're too confused to be much help. But a nice clean jail cell with a bunch of cameras? That thing'll swerve off."

"Why do you think it called you, and not the others?" Franklin asked before Billy turned to go.

"Don't know if it was calling just me or not," Billy said. "But I was the only one who heard it." He shrugged. "Just thought it was another one of those damned voices. Thank you for the water," he said, nodding his head at Darryl. "And thanks for the warning." Then he turned and tramped off through the woods.

"Should we go after him?" Franklin asked Darryl quietly. Was it safe for him here in the woods? How long before that thing came after him again? Or would it go after someone else now?

"Do you want him sleeping on your front porch?" Darryl replied. "'Cause he can't go home with me. You gonna give him a ride on the front of your bicycle?"

Franklin sighed. Darryl was right. He just wished he could do something more.

"He'll be all right," Darryl assured Franklin. "Now, let's get back on the trail."

Franklin let himself be persuaded. Billy would be fine. He'd be able to take care of himself. He'd probably been doing it for a long time.

"Where was that thing standing?" Darryl asked, trying to distract Franklin.

"Right where we are," Franklin told him. "Like a goddamn cloud."

"Let's go rain on its day then," Darryl said.

~

FRANKLIN WAS ready to go home. All the woods looked the same to him at this point—same trees, same brambles, same damn heat and noise. His water was gone, he'd soaked through his clothes with sweat —so bad it was like he'd gone swimming in them. He was sure he had blisters on his toes, on his heels, even on his thighs. And he was going to have to work in the morning.

"Come on, Cuz," Darryl said. "Let's just try it one more time. Go back to Lexine's cabin and search again."

Franklin shook his head. "I'm tired," he complained. Then the woods backed off a little and Franklin walked into an open space. "Is this the clearing where we saw Billy?"

Darryl gave him a look that just said *Duh*.

"Instead of going back to Lexine's, how about we go find where Billy first saw the thing? Go to that hobo camp? "

"That's a good idea," Darryl said. He knelt down next to the spot where they'd found Billy, then stood back up, peering intently. "This way. Come on."

The trail seemed obvious, even to Franklin. His heart lurched when he realized why: Billy had been in worse shape than they'd realized, barely walking straight, breaking branches left and right.

They should have stayed with him, or gotten him some help, or maybe a lift into town, or something.

Darryl walked faster. Was he feeling as guilty as Franklin?

They smelled the camp before they saw it, the wind carrying the stink of unwashed men. It was just four of them, camped in a gully, surrounded by pines. Two of the men lay passed out, their filthy blankets over their faces, while their bare feet and legs stuck out, unprotected. A third man lay curled on his side, around his pack, like he was drowning and it would save him.

The last man sat propped up against a tree. He had a filthy beard but a shaved head. A once white T-shirt rode up on his chest, exposing a fat belly and tied-off pants. He waved at them before taking another swig of something brown in an unmarked bottle.

There wasn't any sign of Billy.

"Excuse me, sir," Franklin said, trying to be as polite as Mama would want him to be. "Do you know where Billy is?"

"Who?" the guy asked. He scratched at his bare belly with his blackened fingernails and belched.

"White guy, brown eyes, hears voices," Darryl said, bored. He reached behind him and drew his gun out of his pack, then held it casually, barrel down.

The guy spit to one side. "He said he was being hounded by the winds from Hell. But he's always saying things like that. The creek's over that way. You might find him there."

"Thank you," Franklin said as they turned to go. "What do you want to bet they'll all be cleared out by the time we get back?" he asked Darryl.

"Pretty safe bet," Darryl said with a grin. "As they should be. Woods aren't safe," he added seriously.

The stream—an offshoot of Wolf River—lay like a black ribbon between the trees. Rocks the size of cars lay casually piled on the bank, as well as across the water.

Billy lay in the middle of the stream, looking like he was sunbathing naked on one of the big rocks.

But this time, they was too late to save him.

～

"SHOULD HAVE KNOWN it'd be you finding the body," Sheriff Thompson told Franklin sourly. They stood out on the blacktop, next to the police cruiser. Though the sun was finally setting, the baked road still held the heat of the day. Bats chittered above them, going to do their duty. The pine scent had died, and the woods felt more ominous as it got darker.

"Me?" Franklin asked. "Why me?" *Shit.* Had the cops figured out he'd been out at Lexine's place?

"Weird stuff happens around you. And your family. I don't like it," the sheriff said, running his finger and thumb along his mustache, stroking it slowly.

"We don't like—" Darryl started hotly.

"Weird stuff happens to lots of families," Franklin countered, interrupting Darryl before he said something that got them both thrown in jail.

The sheriff looked at Darryl, then at Franklin. "I want to see both of you down at the judicial center, in my office, tomorrow morning, first thing."

"Sir, I've got work—" Franklin said.

"I'm sure your boss'll understand." Sheriff Thompson paused. "It isn't just about this. It's about Lexine, as well." His hard piercing eyes bored into Franklin.

Damn it. Should he just confess that he was there? Get it over with?

"All right. We'll be there," Darryl said, grabbing Franklin's arm. "Can we go?"

"Yeah," the sheriff said. "See you in the morning."

Franklin and Darryl turned back up the road, going the long way back up to Lexine's cabin, where Darryl's truck and Franklin's bike were still parked. It would have been shorter going through the woods, but even Darryl was hesitant to go back into that darkness.

"Want to tell me what the hell is going on with you?" Darryl asked once they'd walked far enough up the road to be out of earshot.

"What do you mean?" Franklin asked, startled.

"You were leaking guilt like a sieve," Darryl stated. "What were you going to confess back there?"

Franklin sighed. He could tell Darryl, right? "I was out in Lexine's cabin. The morning the cops found her. I was in the cabin when I heard the sirens. That first trail we followed? That was me, high-tailing it outta there."

"Shit."

They trudged on for a bit in silence.

"I should just tell them," Franklin said.

"No. You should not. You don't ever tell any cop anything about your business," Darryl said adamantly.

"Then there's the corn," Franklin added.

"What corn?"

"Didn't the cops tell you? I'd thought they'd told the family," Franklin said. At Darryl's blank look, Franklin continued. "They found cobs of corn next to Lexine's body."

"What the hell?" Darryl asked. "How'd they get there?"

"One of my ghosts," Franklin confessed. "Normally, a ghost can't lift something that heavy. I don't know how she managed it. Then to travel there with them—no idea."

"Are they from your crop?" Darryl asked.

Franklin shook his head. "I've checked. I don't see nothing missing."

"Then where's this ghost of yours getting them from?"

Franklin sighed. "Karl Metzger."

"Wait, the guy who's always beating you at the state fair?"

"I'm surprised you remember his name," Franklin said dryly. "But yeah. Him. Karl. I think him and the ghost—Gloria—they had something. Maybe." He still didn't know if Karl had loved Gloria or not, but Franklin figured Gloria did care for Karl.

"So she's stealing his corn?" Darryl asked.

"Yeah." Franklin thought for a moment. "You remember what Billy said about getting arrested? That being around a bunch of folks would stop that thing?"

Darryl nodded.

"I was thinking the same thing," Franklin said. "Maybe Gloria's trying to get Karl arrested. I'm wondering now—is that thing going after him next?"

"Shit, I don't know," Darryl said. "You want to go to his farm?"

Franklin hesitated. It was late, now. He and Karl had never been friends, just competitors. "I'll stop by there tomorrow," Franklin said slowly. He'd learned in high school to leave Karl alone—he was a skinny white boy, but fast with his fists, and faster to take insult.

There wasn't a chance in hell that Karl would believe Franklin that there might be some crazed spirit coming after him, or that he had a ghostly protector. But somehow, Franklin was going to have to convince him otherwise.

CHAPTER 6

FRANKLIN STARED AT THE SHERIFF. "Are you sure, sir?" He shifted on the hard green-vinyl chair in front of the sheriff's desk. All the long slatted blinds were pulled, hiding the clear day outside. Nothing was out of place: Every paper was filed, all the pens were neatly lined up in the cup on the sheriff's desk, and even the file folders were color coded.

"That's what the coroner told me. Lexine was killed by someone. The scratches and gouges and like that—most of those were post-mortem." Sheriff Thompson paused. "We'd like a set of your fingerprints. We already have Darryl's."

It didn't surprise Franklin that Darryl was in the system.

"Why?" Franklin asked, uncertain. He hadn't killed Lexine. And while his prints were certain to be in the cabin—he'd visited there more than once—so were most of the family's.

"The killer left behind his handprint around Lexine's neck," the sheriff said. "It would just be to rule you out as a suspect."

"I didn't do it," Franklin said. "And why don't you compare the handprint to that businessman? Earl Jackson? Didn't he do it?"

"We're still investigating," the sheriff said. He glared at Franklin. "I'd think you'd want to be cleared."

"I didn't do it," Franklin repeated. "And I don't want my prints in the system."

Shit. He shouldn't have said that.

"Why not?" Sheriff Thompson asked. "What are you trying to hide?"

"Nothing, sir," Franklin said. Fresh sweat broke out all across his shoulders. "I've always tried to steer clear of the law. You don't really need my prints. You just want 'em."

The sheriff's eyes narrowed. "I don't know what your cousin's been telling you, and I don't care what you've seen on TV. I'm not out to get you, or to make up something against you."

"Then why do you need my prints? Really?" Franklin insisted. "Because if she was killed by something human, it had to be Jackson."

"There's all that corn," the sheriff pointed out.

"So take a cob from my field and compare it," Franklin said.

"Karl Metzger accuses you of stealing his crop. He thinks your fingerprints will be all over those cobs," Sheriff Thompson said, staring right at Franklin.

"I didn't steal those cobs," Franklin said adamantly. At least he knew he was telling the truth about that.

"Then who did?"

Franklin wasn't gonna tell the sheriff about Gloria. "Don't know," he lied. "But it wasn't me. And you got no cause asking for my prints. Not unless Karl files a complaint. And he has no proof, 'cause I didn't do it."

"I'm going to find something, you know," the sheriff said. "Just be warned. And when I do, I'll get a court order, and I'll haul your ass out of that grocery store in front of everyone to get your prints."

"Then that's just what you'll have to do," Franklin said, stubbornly. "Because I didn't do it, I wasn't there, and I don't want you to have my prints just to satisfy your suspicion. Sir."

"I'd have thought you'd be the smart one in your family," the sheriff said as he leaned forward. He folded his hands and stared at Franklin from across the desk. "I think you're hiding something. I don't know what. I don't buy the gossip about ghosts or your family's history. I think you're touched, and not in a good way. And I keep wondering when you'll snap and kill someone."

"I didn't kill Lexine," Franklin repeated.

"So you keep saying," Sheriff Thompson said. "But we're still investigating."

"What about Billy?" Franklin asked. They didn't want his prints for something to do with him, did they?

"Who?"

"The tramp out in the woods."

"William Blake was his full name. Seemed his parents had a sense of foresight," the sheriff said.

"Huh?" Franklin asked, confused.

"Named him after a crazy poet. Seems like they were prophetic, as he ended up just as crazy, always hearing voices."

"So he was special," Franklin said. *Like me. Like Lexine. Like Adrianna.*

"No, just crazy." Sheriff Thompson stroked his mustache, thinking. "I can't compel you for your prints. But I think it'd be smart to volunteer them."

Franklin shook his head. "No sir, I don't think it'd be smart at all."

The silence stretched on between them, anticipation growing in Franklin, like waiting for that first kernel of corn to pop after heating up the lard.

"Can I go?" Franklin finally asked when it seemed the sheriff wasn't going to say anything, ever.

"Yeah, you can. But I've got my eye on you," the sheriff warned. "Any funny stuff going on, and I'll know about it."

"I can believe it, sir," Franklin said as he stood and started walking toward the door.

"Want to tell me why Darryl had rock salt in his rounds?" Sheriff Thompson asked when Franklin reached the door.

"You won't believe me," Franklin said.

"Try me."

"We was hunting the thing that made the scratches. The gouges in Lexine's body. That we'd thought killed Lexine."

"You're right, I don't believe you," the sheriff said.

Franklin paused for another moment, but nothing more was coming from the sheriff. He let himself out, but didn't breathe easily again until he'd left the building, and was walking his bike down Main Street, to the Kroger.

Should he have told the sheriff he'd been at the cabin that day? It felt like it was too late now for him to say anything.

It didn't matter. He hadn't done anything wrong.

All he had to do was convince the sheriff of that.

FRANKLIN RODE wearily from the Kroger, across town, to Karl Metzger's house. Traffic was surprisingly heavy for a Tuesday afternoon. He didn't want to talk with Karl, but he had no choice. The afternoon's heat pressed against Franklin, making his uniform scratch across his back. Four semis passed Franklin on the highway, almost blowing him off the road, making his arms shake and his heart fall down into his belly with fear.

As Franklin expected, Gloria stood waiting for him at the bottom of the driveway up to Karl's house. She glared at him, her arms crossed tightly across her ample bosom, her blond curls shiny in the late afternoon sunshine.

Karl's crops were growing well. The corn was tasseled and gleaming. Franklin suspected that Karl's crop would give him a run for the money yet again this year. But Franklin's crop was coming in earlier that year than Karl's, so he'd have more time to experiment with drying the cobs in the oven, getting each kernel to the perfect consistency.

The big old black Chevy still sat in the driveway near the house, only this time with the hood raised. Karl was nearly bent in two, reaching for something inside.

Franklin got off his bike and walked over to the side of the car. And waited. Karl didn't pause what he was doing or look up. Maybe Karl didn't know Franklin was there? Franklin cleared his throat.

"I seen you already, coming up the drive," Karl commented, still only showing Franklin his backside. "Just a sec."

Franklin waited, shifting restlessly from one foot to the other. He didn't see Gloria, though she'd walked with him up to the car. Karl's vegetables were doing better than Lexine's. What was his secret?

"Knew you'd be coming up here sooner or later," Karl said as he finally finished with his adjustments. He picked up a greasy rag sitting on the edge of the hood to wipe his hands.

Karl was still as skinny as he'd been in high school, but Franklin could also see the muscles along his arms, under his black T-shirt. His blue eyes blazed underneath his brown bushy eyebrows. He wore a neatly trimmed mustache and goatee, something new since high school, and his long brown hair tied back. Though Darryl was a hick, Karl was the perfect image of a good ol' boy.

"Look, I'm sorry about the cops," Franklin said. "I didn't mean for them to come bothering you."

"They wasn't a bother. I was able to show 'em what you—or someone you've hired—has been doing to my crop."

"What do you mean?" Franklin asked. "What has someone been doing?" Was Gloria doing more than just stealing Karl's corn? Was this spirit also doing something?

"I'll show you. Come on." Karl walked up to the house and Franklin followed.

The front hallway had a thick bristle mat that Karl used to clean off the bottoms of his shoes. He pointed to it when he finished, expecting Franklin to do the same. Franklin scuffed his shoes against the rug, exasperated. What did Karl think Franklin had on the bottom of his shoes?

Rich brown hardwood floors led from the entranceway. A steep staircase was on the left. Karl walked past it, down a closed-in hall, to the dining room.

Franklin paused in the doorway. Blue ribbons from the Kentucky State Fair covered the wooden sideboard. Franklin felt sick. He'd been happy to win just a single prize. Karl had dozens and dozens. Rage boiled through Franklin, but he tamped down on it. Wouldn't do no one no good for him to start yelling.

An antique table made of light wood sat in the center of the room. Karl walked around the table and pointed to the corner. Franklin followed, keeping his distance.

A stack of corn cobs lay there, maybe two dozen.

"Every day or so, your thief adds another cob to the pile," Karl said sourly.

"Karl, I ain't been doing this," Franklin said angrily. He walked over to the stacked corn and picked up a cob, peeling back a bit of the husk. It wasn't ripe, which was a shame. The kernels had grown so straight and firm. It would have been good popping corn, if it'd been allowed to mature.

Franklin didn't let himself smile at the thought that maybe Karl was losing the best of his crop. Franklin didn't want to win because Karl wasn't showing his best at the fair.

Gloria appeared just behind Karl's shoulder, looking longingly at him.

"Did you ever know someone named Gloria?" Franklin asked.

"Who?" Karl asked, confused.

"Gloria," Franklin repeated.

Karl shook his head, his face blank.

Oh hell. Did Gloria just love Karl from afar? Did they not even know each other? This was gonna get real ugly. How the hell was he supposed to resolve a love affair that hadn't even been real?

"Karl, think," Franklin said, impatient. "Pretty black woman, dyed blond hair—curled—red nails and lips?" Franklin wasn't about to mention how Gloria was dressed.

Karl looked down at the ground. "She cut my hair," he said quietly. "At your mama's salon."

Franklin hadn't ever met Gloria, which meant she'd started sometime after Mama had died and Franklin had stopped going to the salon. "Did you two go out?"

Karl shook his head. "But I wanted to ask her out. I was planning on it. Had bought the tickets to the opera house and everything. Then she got herself killed in that bus crash on the Interstate. You know, last week? Week before?"

"Is she mad at you, Karl?" Franklin asked.

"She didn't even know I existed," Karl said with some heat. "So you can just forget about whatever you were about to say."

"She knew, Karl," Franklin said. "She's the one stealing your crop."

"Yeah, right, pull the other one." When Franklin didn't smile or laugh, but continued to look serious, Karl said, "All right. That's it. Leave."

"She's trying to help you," Franklin said as he headed toward the door. "I don't know why she's stealing your crop. But she ain't trying to get revenge."

"Bullshit," Karl said. "That's all women know."

Gloria transferred her glare to Karl.

"Shouldn't have said that, Karl," Franklin said.

"I don't believe in your ghosts. I think it's you, or some kid you've hired to steal my corn. And I'm gonna prove it, too. I'm gonna get my shotgun, fill it with rock salt, and stay up all night in the corn field."

Gloria tipped her head back, opened her mouth, and howled. Just the sight of her raised all the hair on the back of Franklin's neck. He was damned glad he couldn't actually hear any noise: It likely would have broken a window or two.

As far as Gloria was concerned, if Karl spent the night in his field, he'd get himself killed. Franklin remembered that silent watcher the one time he'd been in Karl's field, the way it had set his back up. Was there something waiting for Karl out in his fields?

Something deadly?

And there was nothing Franklin could do about it.

～

AFTER LEAVING KARL'S PLACE, Franklin rode back into town, straight to the Sorrels' house. He knew he had to call on them before he could go home. There was still a bit of light in the sky, with the high clouds shining pink and purple.

Kids played in the yards and didn't pay Franklin any heed as he rode by. Neighbors talked to each other. It seemed like a perfectly normal summer evening.

But Franklin felt far from normal. Lexine was dead. That damn spirit was going after people he cared about—even Darryl, who he'd figured would be destroyed by alcohol, not some spirit.

How could Franklin protect them? He didn't know if the shots filled with rock salt would work. Would they just anger the spirit? Maybe make it stronger?

It was evil. Maybe he should talk with Preacher Sinclair about fighting evil, though he'd probably just tell Franklin to go read his bible.

Franklin sighed. He missed Mama at times like this. She'd have known what to do.

No new art hung out front on the Sorrel's fence. Franklin wondered if they'd been outside the yard at all since the attack. He rang the doorbell on the fence. The chime had changed: instead of a regular *ding-dong,* now it rang like church bells.

Ray opened the gate door after just a bit. "Franklin, good to see you," he said, reaching out and shaking Franklin's hand. "I'm sorry for your loss. Come on in."

Inside the fence, three more twisting white-rock roads had been added since Franklin's last visit. They led from various parts of the yard to the tree men. "Adrianna's insistent on giving them more power," Ray said quietly.

It looked like a spider's web painted by a child.

"Franklin!" Adrianna called from where she was seated. "Come and have some sweet tea."

It looked like she was having a late-night dinner, seated on a blanket under her tree men statues.

Except that next to her was a camp stove that looked as though it had been set up for days, now. Three wooden shelves, supported by cinder blocks and covered with pots, pans, and dishes stretched on the other side. Even a suitcase filled with clothes lay open in the camp.

"Hey Miss Adrianna," Franklin said, coming over to sit beside her. "Is everything all right?"

"It's so lovely here! And Ray is doing everything he can to help. Aren't you, dear?"

Ray gave his indulgent smile, though even Franklin could see it was strained. "Yep. Anything for my girl."

"I'm so sorry to hear about your cousin," Adrianna said after she handed Franklin a tall cup filled with ice and sweet tea.

"Thank you, ma'am," Franklin said. "It's a great loss." It still made his heart hurt to think about it.

"Was it that creature that killed her?" Ray asked.

"The police think she was killed by a man. Maybe the businessman she was found with. But the creature was there too. Scratched her and the businessman all up." Franklin didn't bother to mention his own troubles with the police.

"I had lunch with Earl while he was here," Ray admitted.

"Do the cops know?" Franklin asked, concerned. What would Sheriff Thompson say if he came over here and saw Adrianna's nest?

"Yeah, they called, and I went in to give a statement." Ray sighed. "I don't think Earl killed Lexine, though. He was a business acquaintance of mine."

"What was he doing here?" Franklin asked.

"Looking to set up a high-powered retreat. Not a resort, not like what tourists would use. But a place to escape from everything. Really high priced, too. It would have been a great success," Ray said. "Earl came out here to see if the economy could support it, how much would have to be flown in, how much could a resort tend to itself."

"Ray—was Earl special? In any way?" Franklin asked. "Like Miss Adrianna?"

"Not that I know of, no," Ray said, shaking his head. "But he did have a nose for making money. That man lost and made more fortunes than most people can even dream about."

"There's more to life than just money," Adrianna said solemnly.

"Unless you don't have enough," Ray pointed out gently. "Anyway. I figure he went out to Lexine's to see about buying some of her land."

"Lexine would never have sold," Franklin said.

"Not even for a pot full of money? I mean, a seriously stupid amount?" Ray asked.

"Miss Adrianna, would you move from here?" Franklin turned and asked. "Away from your power lines and this nest?"

"Not for any amount of money. Not now that I've settled in and can see everything." Adrianna sighed. "I hate to say it, but I think that creature's awful attack was useful. I didn't see as well before as I do now."

"I figure Lexine felt the same way, chose that spot because it amplified her power, and wouldn't have ever moved from it," Franklin said.

"Still, Earl wouldn't have killed her for it. He would have found other land, some other way to make the money," Ray said.

"The cops believe something human killed her. Left his handprint around her neck," Franklin said.

"Do you think Earl found her that way, and was trapped there? That his death was circumstantial? What exactly killed him?" Adrianna asked.

"I don't know," Franklin said, frowning. "Maybe the same human killed both of them."

"So maybe the creature is under the control of something living," Ray said. "He kills, then it feeds."

Franklin rolled his eyes. "That's far too complicated. No, I think the spirit is exactly what it is, an evil spirit. It views us—people who are special—as rival predators." He explained catching a glimpse of the thing when he and Darryl had been hunting it, along with how it had killed Billy.

"So it has killed," Ray said thoughtfully. He looked with worry over at Adrianna.

"Now stop," Adrianna said, patting Ray's thigh affectionately. "It can't get to us here."

Ray looked around the garden, then, with longing, back at the house.

"Darryl can track this thing," Franklin said. "We just have to figure out what to do with it, once we find it. Then you two should be able to go back to normal."

Now Adrianna looked worried. "Excuse me," she said, standing and walking over to the trunk of one of her tree men, petting it and crooning to it.

The tree branches moved in a wind that Franklin couldn't feel.

Adrianna's power was growing.

He looked over at Ray, who looked resigned. "Wanna go take a walk through the garden? Show me everything else?" Franklin asked.

"Sure," Ray said. They walked over to the far side of the fish pond, close to the house.

"Adrianna's always been...artistic," Ray started. "We moved here when it got too hard for her in LA."

"You miss the city?" Franklin asked.

"God, yes. No offense, but this town was never my idea of a retirement destination, you know?" Ray sighed. "But Adrianna needed someplace slow, and quiet, and she insisted on here. Never quite knew what she saw in this place. Until now."

"What's wrong, Ray?" Franklin asked.

"I'm afraid I'm losing her. To it. To them." He gestured at the tree creatures she'd created. "She says her power's growing—maybe it is, maybe it isn't—but her strangeness sure is. She's different, now."

"I'm sorry," Franklin said. He wasn't sure what he could do to help.

"We weren't able to have kids," Ray continued. "Now, these things—they're like children and grandkids, salvation and savior, all rolled up into one."

Franklin looked back at Adrianna. She stood holding the hand of one of the tree men, swaying and singing softly. The branches above her swayed as well.

If it came to a choice, if the creature came again, would she choose to save Ray? To sacrifice one of her creations for his life?

Franklin just didn't know.

FRANKLIN WEARILY RODE his bike home through the cooling evening. How come dealing with Karl and Adrianna and the sheriff make him feel as though he'd worked really hard all day, hauling bags of rocks or fertilizer or something? Maybe he'd just go home and straight to bed. Once he left town and rode down Stevens Street the temperature dropped even further away from the buildings and into the fields, while the call of the cicadas cycled up higher.

No police car or cousin's truck waited for Franklin in the driveway of his house that evening.

No, what waited for him was much, much worse.

The spirit of Sweet Bess had found her way back to his home. Franklin didn't know why he could see her—he'd only ever been able to see her at Lexine's place. He couldn't normally see spirits.

But Sweet Bess stood there, like a demented guard dog. If she could have made noise, Franklin knew she'd be grunting and snorting at him. Her tiny pig eyes glared red at him, out of her ghostly white skin. She pawed the ground, a sure sign she was about to attack.

Shit. Where could he go? Franklin really wanted to go inside. He was too tired to deal with this mess. However, Sweet Bess stood between him and the door, and didn't look like she was likely to let him pass.

Franklin got off his bike and kept it between him and the glaring sow. At least he wasn't carrying any of her lard.

That led Franklin to a plan. The root cellar had its own entrance, to the side. It would take some time to get the lock open, but so would unlocking the front door, if Sweet Bess was charging him. Maybe if he rode around the house, she'd follow him. Even in death, she couldn't run as fast as he could ride. He could get around the house, maybe go around twice, and leave himself enough time to get through the root cellar door.

Franklin got back on his bike and started peddling around the house. The front wheel bumped over a hose that he hadn't wound back up, across the rocks leading away from the house gutter, onto the thick grass patch that made up the backyard, around the house, then back onto the front gravel driveway.

Sweet Bess followed, but she'd never been fast alive, and death hadn't speeded her up any. By the time Franklin circled the house twice and was back to the root cellar, she was about halfway around the house, still struggling to catch up.

Franklin ditched his bike and fumbled out his keys, reaching for the lock on the cellar door.

Sweet Bess came around the corner, saw what he was doing, and doubled her pace.

It was really gonna hurt when she hit. Franklin jammed the key into the lock, twisted, and pulled. Fortunately, he kept the lock well oiled, and it slid open easily.

With Sweet Bess breathing down his back, Franklin wrenched open one of the cellar doors and leapt down the stairs, panting and sweating.

The sow passed above him. The wooden door groaned loudly as the spirit passed through it, as if had suddenly aged. Franklin shivered. What the hell was Sweet Bess up to? He hoped she wouldn't try to come in the house—she'd never done so when she'd been alive, and he certainly couldn't stop her if she was dead.

What the hell did she want? Why was she bothering him?

Thump. Crash.

What was that? It came from directly above Franklin's head.

Something was in the house.

Cautiously, Franklin poked his head back out the root cellar door. Sweet Bess stood not two feet away, pawing the ground, about to make another run at him. Franklin heaved himself up out of the root cellar, grabbed the door and pulled it shut, the galloping sow on the other side.

He didn't know if it would help, but he put the wooden beam across the doors to lock them. He wouldn't be able to come and go as easily, but hopefully, he wouldn't need to.

Franklin turned back to the dark of the cellar. There wasn't a flashlight in the root cellar, so he got out his phone, using the tiny screen to light his way. Though the floor was clear, he still didn't want to run into one of the walls.

Slowly, Franklin made his way up the basement stairs. "Mama?" Franklin called out.

Thump. Tinkle.

"Gloria?"

Whump.

What the hell was going on? Was that a burglar in his kitchen? Were Ray's crazy theories about a human controlling the spirit actually true?

Franklin turned the doorknob to the kitchen slowly and opened the door a crack.

Chaos reigned in his kitchen.

The creature was there. It whirled like something possessed, snatching up everything not put away and smashing it against the walls, the ceiling, and the ground. It even managed to get into the cupboard holding Franklin's glassware, and was gleefully smashing that as well.

What the hell did that thing want? Just to destroy things? Or was it here to kill Franklin?

Franklin opened the door just a bit more.

For the first time in over a year, Mama wasn't sitting at the kitchen table.

"What the hell?"

The thing paused in its destruction.

Shit. Franklin realized he'd spoken out loud.

Had this spirit killed Mama? She'd been special, too. Did it have the power to kill ghosts?

Before Franklin could go back down the stairs, the spirit grabbed him with its sticky vines.

Franklin cried out—they stung like nettles, cutting into his skin like barbed wire.

The thing threw Franklin up toward the ceiling, then let him fall. Sharp pieces of broken bowls jammed into Franklin's back, while the fall itself pushed all the air from his lungs.

Franklin still scrambled to his feet. Shit. He had to get out of here, or this thing would kill him. Where could he go? What would save him? Maybe he could get out the front door.

However, the thing reached for Franklin again before he could get more than two steps, slicing open his arms and slamming him against the wall. Shaken, Franklin pushed away, trying again for the door.

88

He had to get out of there. Or he was a goner.

Suddenly, Mama was in the kitchen. She stood between the thing and her boy, her *intent* clear: It was going to have to go through her first before it could get at her boy.

The thing obliged. It flayed her with its whips, tearing into her ghostly flesh.

Mama didn't cry out in pain—the dead couldn't make a sound. She stood steady and firm as the mountain of Abraham, bleeding ghostly blood; little trickles of light flowing from her arms.

"Mama!" Franklin cried.

Mama turned and glared at him. *Run, you fool.*

Franklin ran, stumbling out the front door.

Was Mama okay? Would she survive?

He looked around the yard. Sweet Bess was nowhere to be seen.

But Sheriff Thompson's Crown Vic, with the blue and red squad lights on, was pulling into the drive.

CHAPTER 7

"WHAT THE HELL HAPPENED TO YOU?" Sheriff Thompson asked as he hopped out of his car.

"A fight?" Franklin said. He didn't know what else he could say. He couldn't lie and say that nothing had happened. He looked down, his back twinging. Shit. He probably had glass embedded all up and down his spine. His arms had deep gouges in them, bleeding heavily. His shirt was ripped around his torso, and had provided little protection. Now, it stuck to his sides. Damn it. He was gonna have to buy another uniform shirt.

Something clattered inside the house.

"Who's in there, Franklin?" Sheriff Thompson asked. He flicked off the safety on his weapon but didn't pull it out of his holster as he walked up the front porch stairs.

"No one's there," Franklin said, hurrying up behind him.

Would it be better if the sheriff saw the spirit destroying Franklin's kitchen? Or just the aftermath? The sheriff wouldn't believe his eyes if he saw the spirit. But maybe Franklin could explain the destruction.

The sheriff pushed open the door and called out, "Hello?"

Nothing replied.

Sheriff Thompson walked through the hallway into the kitchen.

The spirit was gone, having thrown its fit. Broken dishes and glasses lay scattered in a spiral pattern across the floor. Two of the kitchen chairs were turned over, and the table itself had been shoved into the corner.

Why had that thing attacked Franklin like that? Had it been trying to kill him? That hadn't felt like its *intent*—it had just wanted to hurt Franklin as much as it could. And where was Mama?

The sheriff looked around the kitchen. "You got some explaining to do," he said darkly.

"You won't believe me," Franklin said with a sigh.

Sheriff Thompson glanced over at Franklin, his hard eyes dark in the dim light. "You're right. I probably wouldn't. But I do believe you've been in a pretty bad fight, and you need some stitches."

"I'll be all right," Franklin said. He just needed someone to clean out the glass in his back. He could take care of the rest.

"Franklin, son, I don't think you will be," the sheriff said. "I'd feel much better about doing my civic duty if you'd let me drive you to the hospital."

"That's all the way across the county," Franklin protested.

"All right. How about urgent care, then? There's the country doctor's office in town."

"I'll bleed on your seats. Stain your car," Franklin said, though he knew his protests were getting weaker.

"If it'll make you feel better, I'll let you clean it up later."

Franklin looked around the ruins of his kitchen. He couldn't do anything more here. Mama would either come back or not. And where the hell was Gloria? Had the thing already attacked her and driven her off?

"Come on." The sheriff had Franklin's arm where it wasn't bleeding and was leading him out of the kitchen.

Everything seemed distant suddenly, like there was a bale of cotton between Franklin and the world. "Why's it all so far away?" he asked.

"I think it's shock," the sheriff said. He got a silver emergency blanket—the kind Darryl had put in their backpacks when they'd been hunting—and got Franklin folded into his car. He'd even had to help Franklin pull his legs up. Why weren't they moving right? He worked to find a comfortable way to sit, where he wasn't putting any pressure on his back, and ended up twisted, so his shoulder rested on the seat, while his legs were stretched out to balance him.

"It'll be okay, son," Sheriff Thompson said.

Why did the sheriff sound so worried?

"Don't you be going to sleep on me," the sheriff growled, brushing his hand against Franklin's arm.

Pain spiked through Franklin's system. "Why'd you do that for?" he asked.

"'Cause you can't pass out on me. Not yet," the sheriff insisted.

"Why was you coming out to see me?" Franklin shouted over the wailing sirens the sheriff had turned on. Why were they in such a hurry?

"Karl was mad as a hornet. Insisted I come arrest you. He'd shot something in his field, filled it full of rock salt. Said it must have been someone you'd hired, to ruin his crop."

"Ah—that's why it was so angry," Franklin said. No wonder the spirit had attacked him. But—damn it. That meant rock salt didn't work.

"It?" the sheriff asked.

"Another thing you don't believe in," Franklin said. So much was closed to the sheriff. It was so sad.

But at least since the sheriff was normal, he didn't have to worry about that damn spirit coming after him.

They stopped in short order, or maybe time was a bit funny, in front of the hospital. "You said we'd go to urgent care," Franklin accused the sheriff.

"I lied," Sheriff Thompson said with a grin. "Besides, you really need to be here."

Emergency technicians bundled Franklin out of the car. He tried to answer their questions but the sheriff talked over him, describing his injuries in clinical terms that Franklin couldn't quite hold onto, as well as talking about him going into shock.

As the sheriff passed him off to the technicians, he also instructed them to check for rock salt, just in case.

〜

FRANKLIN WOKE, stiff and sore, in a strange room that was all white. Shit. Had he died?

No, he remembered now. He was in the hospital. Thick padded bandages covered the gouges on his arms, and he couldn't feel his back: It was like someone had shot it full of Novocain. Something was stuck into his bandaged left hand, a needle leading to a tube leading to a bag of some clear fluid—saline, maybe.

Damn it. How the hell was he going to afford this? The room smelled like sour medicine and stinky bleach. A white curtain hung along one side, blocking Franklin's view of the rest of the room. A TV hung on the wall at the foot of the bed.

Franklin pressed the call button, hoping that he wasn't going to have to pay for every nurse's visit.

A young white girl poked her head into the room. "Good to see you awake," she said, stepping further into the room. "I'm Julie. You're at Wesley County hospital." She had brown, shoulder-length hair that looked as though it'd be soft to touch, and big hazel eyes over a tiny nose dusted with freckles.

"When can I get out?" Franklin asked as he sat up.

Okay, sitting up maybe was a bit of a mistake, as the room swam. But Franklin stubbornly stayed sitting, not supported by the pillows, even though the pretty nurse came quickly over to his side and pushed gently on his shoulder.

"You should just rest, sir," she insisted. "You've lost a lot of blood."

"You should've seen the other guy," Franklin weakly joked. He resisted Nurse Julie for another few moments before he finally lay back. Then he remembered. "Why don't my back hurt?" he asked.

"You're on morphine," Julie told him. "As well as antibiotics. Whatever attacked you left a nasty infection behind."

"When can I get out?" Franklin asked again. "Not that I want to leave a pretty girl like you," he added. "But I gotta get back home." He had such a mess to clean up there. Plus, a funeral to go to. And he somehow had to stop anyone else from being attacked.

"I understand," the nurse said with a smile. "You got a wife at home to get to, right?"

Franklin chuckled. "No, ma'am. Just family and a farm."

"Speaking of family and friends, is there anyone you want to call? The phone's right here."

"I'd like to be able to tell them when they can come and get me," Franklin hinted.

"I'll go get the doctor and we'll see about getting you released," Nurse Julie said. "Then I'll come back in and give you instructions on how to clean and change your bandages. You'll need help," she added. "Backs are tricky, and it's difficult to do arms too, sometimes."

"One of my cousins will help," Franklin said, though he wasn't sure which one.

"That's so nice to have family," Julie said.

"What time is it?" Franklin asked. It still seemed light out—was it only mid-afternoon?

"5:45 AM," the nurse said cheerfully.

"Have you been up all night?" Franklin asked. "You still look like you're full of energy."

"Thank you," Julie said. "I'm just used to it. I am about to go off shift, though. So let me get you a doctor before *he* goes off shift, and we'll see if we can't get you out of here."

"Thanks," Franklin said as Julie left the room.

What had happened to him? Franklin shook his head. He didn't remember much of anything after the doctors had first numbed his back so they could take the glass out. He should have just been in and out, that's what they said, outpatient, right? Nothing about having to stay overnight.

Was this some kind of effect of the creature? Was this why Adrianna had gotten more spacey? Was Franklin going off the deep end now? As if his life wasn't hard enough already.

With a sigh, Franklin turned on the TV, looking for the weather report. More of the recent heat wave was predicted. Of course. He wasn't going to catch a break.

∼

Darryl came to get Franklin. He agreed to bring Franklin's suit as well, after stopping by the house.

Franklin was ready to be out of there. The new nurse wasn't as cute or friendly as Julie had been. And the paperwork had been horrible. At least his insurance covered a lot of it—but he was still out a huge chunk of change.

"I'll help you clean up," Darryl told Franklin as he handed over the clothes. "That thing did a right good job of messing up everything at your place."

"It's kind of poisonous, too," Franklin said. "Doctor said my cuts was all infected. Every single one of them." Part of why he was so fuzzy about the night before was because they'd been feeding him high octane antibiotics. The doctors had been afraid it was some sort of staph infection.

Franklin took his clothes into the bathroom to change. It wasn't easy pulling on his clean white shirt over his bandaged arms. His legs weren't much better: Though they hadn't been gouged by the creature, they'd still been scratched up the previous day when he went running through the woods. It was part of why the doctors had been concerned—the infection from his arms and back had spread to his legs as well.

Franklin finally admitted defeat and came back out into the hospital room. Darryl was perched on the bed, flipping through TV channels.

"Can you help?" Franklin asked, holding out his suit coat. He just couldn't get his arm moved around to catch the sleeve. The drugs were starting to wear off, too, and trying to do even normal stuff just set his back off.

Darryl silently helped Franklin into his jacket. At least Franklin could slip on his shoes, didn't have to tie them: He wasn't sure he could reach down to get at the laces.

They got the prescription filled at hospital, and Franklin dry-swallowed two of the pain pills right away. He knew he'd be high as a kite, but his back was already starting to ache.

The drive to Katherinesville was hell. Franklin tried to stay twisted in the seat, just have his shoulder resting against it, as he had in the sheriff's car, but it didn't seem to work as well. He felt every bump like a jolt from a cattle prod.

People were already gathered outside the church for the funeral. Franklin was going to have to get his whole suit dry cleaned since he was sweating so much already, before they stepped into the bright sunshine.

"Come on," Darryl said, taking Franklin by the arm and steering him away from the front. "Let's go in the back."

Franklin gladly followed. He liked people, but he felt vulnerable today, not sure he wanted to see much of anyone except family. Or maybe, just his bed.

From the back entrance they went straight to the fireside room, next to the sanctuary, where the rest of the family was all gathered.

Aunt Jasmine sat on one of the floral couches, crying quietly into her kerchief. Preacher Sinclair, in his purple robes, sat beside her. She wore her best red suit, complete with hat and gloves. It broke Franklin's heart so see such a proud mountain of a woman shaking with such grief.

Franklin was surprised to see Lexine's father there—after he'd left, he'd had nothing to do with any of the family. He stood to one side, all alone, looking uncomfortable in his fancy rose-colored suit.

May was at least decently covered in a navy blue dress, and her eyes were clear as she handed her mother another tissue. Jason entertained the kids in another corner, sitting on the floor with them and telling them a story.

Franklin sat down on one of the side chairs, near his aunt. He felt like collapsing with pain and grief, swallowing down the lump in his throat. It was just so unfair that Lexine had passed on.

May left her mother's side and came to crouch down next to Franklin. "You look like shit," she said quietly.

"You should see the other guy," Franklin said, repeating his joke.

"What happened?" May asked. "Darryl just said he had to go pick you up at the hospital. Details. Now. I want the dirt. Who'd you get into a fight with?"

Franklin sighed. "No dirt. No real fight. Just a stupid angry spirit. The same one as killed Lexine." Even though the police thought it was the businessman, Franklin knew the real killer was the creature. It had damn near killed him. It might have killed Mama, if you could kill a ghost.

"Shit," May said loudly. Everyone looked at her. "Excuse me, reverend," May said contritely. "My cousin here's been attacked by the same thing that killed Lexine."

Franklin closed his eyes for a moment. *Damn it.* She shouldn't have just announced it like that. When he opened his eyes again, everyone was staring at him.

"Is that true?" Aunt Jasmine demanded.

"The thing that left the gouges in Lexine's face," Franklin said, trying to at least clarify what he meant. "Yeah. It attacked me. Put me in the hospital last night."

Aunt Jasmine turned a baleful glare at Preacher Sinclair. "Preacher, what are you gonna do about this thing?"

"Me?" the preacher asked. "I'm not sure why you think I should get involved." His dark skin couldn't hide how he paled at the thought.

"Didn't you say this thing is evil?" Aunt Jasmine said, turning toward Darryl.

"That's what the tramp said." Darryl asked. "Franklin? What would you say?"

"Its *intent* is to kill," Franklin said quietly. "It's a predator. It sees anyone who's special as competition. But…it also likes to cause pain." He shivered, remembering how helpless he'd felt in the face of its fury and hate.

"See?" Aunt Jasmine said. "An evil creature that likes to cause pain, that's not of this world. Should be right up your alley, preacher."

"I'll see what I can do," Preacher Sinclair said. "We'll talk, after the funeral," he added, nodding at Franklin.

Great. Another day spent hunting in the woods, searching for a creature Franklin wasn't sure he wanted to find. Just what he needed.

～

FRANKLIN SAT BACK DOWN with relief after finishing the hymn,

"There is Power in the Blood." He couldn't believe how standing for even a short while left him tired and aching.

Preacher Sinclair started, leaning on his pulpit, in his purple robes and long white scarf. "Lexine was a child of God, called back to him too soon. Maybe he needed her back by his side, or maybe she needed to be carried for a while."

While Aunt Jasmine was nodding, Franklin shook his head. Lexine had been a strong-willed woman who'd stood on her own two feet for a good long time. She didn't need anyone to take care of her.

Most everything the preacher said, Franklin disagreed with: She'd never finished high school, but she'd been one of the smartest people Franklin knew; she hadn't kept a garden because it was simple or uncomplicated, no, but because it was part of the cycle, life and death, growth and harvest.

Finally, Preacher Sinclair stopped his stomping around the front of the church and called for people from the congregation to say a few words.

Aunt Jasmine was too torn up to say anything, so Darryl got up first, and talked about Lexine's fire and how she'd whooped his ass, more than once. May talked about how Lexine liked to get crazy with her sometimes, and the trouble they'd cause. Jason told about Lexine's gentle side, a part of her that she didn't show many folks.

Finally, they all turned to Franklin, and he realized they expected him to get up and say something. He swayed when he stood, and fresh sweat broke out across his shoulders. The painkillers made him woozy, but he still walked tall to the front and stood behind the reading lectern.

"Lexine was special," Franklin said. "She knew God's spirit, and offered comfort to those who needed it, shelter until they could move on. She followed God's will—though maybe not all his commandments." That brought a chuckle. "She was strong and crazy good and lived such a big life, all the time. I'm gonna miss her, so much."

That was about all Franklin could say. As he walked back to his pew, a light flared at the back of the church, something warm and welcoming. It wasn't a spirit or a ghost, though it had that kind of feeling to it.

Maybe it was just Lexine saying *thank you.*

∾

AFTER THE FUNERAL, everyone gathered in the community room downstairs. The church ladies served punch for the kids, sweet tea and coffee for the adults, along with fresh-baked cookies. The back doors were wide open so the kids could run in and out of the room, despite the heat of the day.

Darryl helped Franklin shed his jacket, though Franklin didn't roll up his sleeves—he didn't want anyone getting a better look at his wounds. He felt vulnerable enough as it was. He sat at one of the round tables covered with the good, white-linen tablecloths, sipping his ice tea. He kept his back to the wall, where it'd be protected, and people wouldn't bang into it by accident.

A pretty white woman with brown hair and hazel eyes came up to him. She wore a bright yellow dress. "Mr. Kanly?" she asked. "That was beautiful, what you said about Lexine. And you're right. She was very, very special."

The woman seemed so familiar. "Nurse Julie!" Franklin finally exclaimed.

"That's right! I wasn't sure you'd remember me. You were kind of out of it."

"Of course I'd remember a pretty nurse like you," Franklin said. "How did you know Lexine?"

"We belonged to the same…group," Julie said.

"What kind of group?" Franklin asked, curious. What did Lexine have to do with a pretty nurse all the way over on the far side of the county?

"It's a group who get together to do good works," Julie said seriously. "Not like a charity, but to pray for the world, sometimes."

Franklin hadn't known Lexine was the praying type. "Really?" he asked. "I hadn't known about it."

"Lexine wouldn't have talked about it to anyone in your family.

She did say that she might have invited you along, sometime, though." Julie paused. "I didn't realize, until I saw you get up at the service, that you were the cousin Franklin that Lexine had talked about."

"So it's like a prayer circle?" Franklin asked. He didn't want to join anything like that: He had enough to deal with already.

"Not exactly," Julie said. She looked over her shoulder to make sure no one was listening too closely. "We're a group of pagans."

FRANKLIN WASN'T sure how he felt about Lexine being in a pagan group. Though she'd never been a church-going kind of lady, Franklin had never had any doubts about her being a good person.

But maybe she'd been getting too close to her spirits if she'd started believing in things beyond her spirits, like other gods and such.

Franklin hadn't ever had any problems with his faith. It'd always been his duty to help ghosts move on to Heaven, if that's where they was headed, to get closer to God.

"So you'll come? To our service for Lexine?" Julie asked. The noise in the community room had died down some, as people were starting to say their goodbyes and final condolences to the family.

"Yes, I'll come," Franklin said. They weren't witches, she'd assured him. But they didn't believe in the God he did.

"Good!" Julie said. "It'll be Saturday night. I'll come and pick you up, because you shouldn't be driving yourself yet."

After pocketing Franklin's address, carefully written out on a napkin, Julie stood up to go. "I think you'll like our group. Maybe feel at home there. I know Lexine did."

"I'm sure I will," Franklin assured Julie, though he wasn't sure at all. Lexine had sworn the only place she ever felt at home was in her cabin in the woods, far away from everyone, surrounded by nature.

After Julie had gone, Franklin thought about getting another iced tea. He knew he'd be expected to go back to Aunt Jasmine's house, to be with the family, but really, he just wanted to go take a nap. It was about time for him to take another set of pain pills as well.

Preacher Sinclair came to sit at Franklin's table just as he was fishing out one of the prescription bottles from his jacket pocket. The preacher had taken off his purple clergy robes and just wore a white dress shirt, with a bright blue and purple striped tie, and light gray slacks.

"I'm sorry to see you in such pain," the preacher started with. "Both your physical and mental anguish."

"Thank you, sir," Franklin replied. "I'll be all right, though." He just needed a couple days rest, or so the doctors had assured him.

"So what exactly happened? What attacked you?" Preacher Sinclair asked. "I'd thought it was some kind of wild animal who got Lexine. She did live pretty far out in the woods."

"It weren't no animal," Franklin said. "It was a creature—a spirit."

"A spirit? Like a devil? Or a demon?"

Franklin shook his head. "I don't think so. It's not from Hell—it's just—not human.

"I see," the preacher said. "And why do you believe that?"

Franklin blinked, trying to come up with something other than the truth, but he was too tired, too doped up on pain killers. "Because I saw it. Gray, like a dust devil, with long black whips, like barbed wire, wrapped around it. It's evil, reverend. I could feel its *intent*. It means to kill me, and anyone else like me."

"Are you sure, son?" Preacher Sinclair asked. "Grief can make people see and do a lot of strange things. I speak from experience, from when I lost my dear wife, years ago. The devil came visiting me every night."

Franklin doubted it was the devil—just the preacher's pain. "I'm sure," he said, then added dryly, "I didn't give myself these injuries, you know."

The preacher chuckled. "I've heard folks talking about you, too. That you can see things like ghosts."

"Yes, sir," Franklin said. "I generally just see ghosts though. Humans who have died and need help passing on."

"To where?" Preacher Sinclair asked.

"To Heaven. They've not been fearful," Franklin said. "They've just needed to settle their business here on earth so they could move forward."

"Interesting," the preacher said. "And you think you'll be able to help this spirit pass along?"

"God willing," Franklin said. He had to stop this thing somehow. Rock salt weren't doing it, but he didn't know what they could use.

"I see. Well, then, I suppose we're going to have to spend some time together." the preacher said. "See if you can show me this spirit."

"It's dangerous," Franklin warned. He had the stitches to prove it.

"I am a man of God," Preacher Sinclair said. "My faith will protect me."

And maybe it would—because little else seemed to work against this thing.

CHAPTER 8

MAY RODE BACK TO FRANKLIN'S farm with Darryl, instead of going to Aunt Jasmine's. "Ma's got enough support for now," May said. "She don't need me until later. I'll go next week, have dinner with her a couple of nights. Bring the kids, give her something to yell about."

Franklin nodded, barely awake. The pain meds had helped his back and arms feel better, but now, he could hardly keep his eyes open. Hopefully, Mama would be waiting for him back in the kitchen by the time he got back home.

They bounced across the road and into Franklin's driveway. The house sat quiet and abandoned, even the fields looking dry in the dusty heat of the day. Sweet Bess wasn't anywhere to be seen.

Had she been trying to warn him off, before? Keep him out of the house while that thing was there?

Franklin's heart just about hit his shoes as he stepped into the kitchen. It was a right mess. Dishes broken and scattered, glass everywhere, and the shards painted with his blood.

But more importantly, no ghosts was waiting for him.

May peeked over his shoulder, *tsked*, and said, "Sweet Jesus." She looked critically at Franklin. "You go lay down before you fall over. Darryl and I can handle this."

"Are you sure?" Franklin asked. "You don't need to. You could go home—"

"Henry'll take care of the kids, and as I said, Ma don't need me right now. You do. Go to bed." May looked at Darryl. "Now, I know you're about as useful as tits on a frog. So you're gonna do exactly what I say, and we'll get this place cleaned before you know it."

Franklin kind of wanted to stay and see that.

"Go," May ordered, pointing toward the back.

Franklin obeyed, slipping into the quiet sanctuary of his room. He pulled down the shades and lay down on the bed, trying to find a comfortable position to lay in. He finally found one propped up on his side, and he slid into a deep, dreamless sleep.

When Franklin awoke, evening had settled in around the house. Dim light pressed against his drawn shades. He couldn't hear anything, and wondered if his cousins had left.

He took a deep breath, and regretted it. Damn, that hurt. He was probably way overdue for his pain meds. But he felt refreshed in a way that he hadn't that morning, and while the pain was sharp, it also slid away cleanly. He knew he was already on the mend.

Franklin slowly rolled out of bed, taking care as he stood up, but the room didn't shift or sway. He opened the shades and looked out on his popping corn. Crap. Looked like something had blown down three of the stalks on the end. Had it been the creature? Gloria? Or maybe even Sweet Bess, who could be a demon when she put her mind to it?

With a sigh, Franklin left his room. He was surprised to see May still sitting there, sunk into the ancient green couch, watching TV with the sound turned down way low. She'd changed out of her funeral clothes and into an old, green T-shirt and cut-off jean shorts.

"'Bout time you got up," May grumbled as she stood up.

"You didn't have to stay," Franklin protested.

"You gonna change those bandages on your back all by your lonesome?" May asked.

"Uhmmm," Franklin said. He hadn't thought of that, though now he remembered Julie mentioning it.

"Yeah, that's what I thought. Let's get those bandages changed, then I'm going home. Darryl'll be by tomorrow to do them the next time. Doctor said three days, right?" May said, steering Franklin toward the guest bathroom, next to what had been Mama's room.

It was as tiny as Franklin's bathroom, but he'd cleaned it up from when it had been Mama's personal grooming station and there had been lotions and creams and gels and stacks of nail polish and four different curling irons and three straighteners and every product and gizmo known to woman. It still carried the overly sweet scent of all that, only much fainter now.

"He did," Franklin said. "How did you know?" He didn't remember telling Darryl, and he sure as shit hadn't told May.

"That nurse, I think her name was Julie? Caught up with me at the funeral. Now, sit, and take off your shirt," May directed Franklin, using a matter-of-fact tone.

Why wasn't May teasing Franklin about Julie? Surely she'd seen them sitting together. Franklin sat on the closed commode wedged between the sink and the shower, then slowly unbuttoned his dress shirt. He should have changed out of it after the funeral, but he'd been too sleepy.

May helped Franklin drag the shirt off, then gave a low whistle. "Dang, Cuz, you really hit the ground hard." She lightly pushed his head to one side. "Shoulda landed on this instead. Would've done less damage."

"Maybe so," Franklin said, relaxing.

May worked quickly and professionally, peeling off the old bandages and taping fresh gauze down, starting with his back, then doing his arms.

"Where'd you learn to do this?" Franklin asked quietly, not wanting to disturb his cousin or the quiet mood that had descended on both of them.

"Studied to be an EMT once," May said. "Never wanted to be a nurse, no goody two shoes. But scraping folks off the highway always sounded like fun."

"Really?" Franklin said. He'd had no idea. "What happened?"

"Carlie, my baby," May admitted. "Not that I would've graduated or anything. I was just farting around, mostly."

"You're good at this," Franklin said quietly. "Maybe when the kids get older, you could go back."

"Maybe," May said. "But then, chances are, they'll be having babies."

"And you could be the cool grandma who saves people's lives," Franklin pointed out.

May grinned at him. "Never could stay away from danger, you know. Always rushing in—"

"When the sane folks are rush out. I remember," Franklin said. Mama had said that about May, more than once, and also that she had more courage than brains.

Franklin didn't know what Mama would say about his injuries. The gouges were puffy around the stitches holding the skin together. He'd have scars on both his arms, and probably his back as well.

"All set," May said as she finished with the last bandage. "Now you," she said, pointing at him, making him want to lean back. "Don't be doing anything stupid. The doctors did a good job with these stitches, but that don't mean you can't rip them out pretty easy. You *rest*. You hear me?"

"Yes, ma'am," Franklin said meekly.

"Lord, why can't I teach that to my kids?" May said with a laugh. "Y'all gonna have to come over some night and show 'em what manners really are."

"I'm sure they know," Franklin said. "But they probably won't use 'em until they've left the house and the world shows 'em they have to."

"When you'd get to be so wise?" May asked, with a grin. "You want help getting into a new shirt?"

Franklin thought for a moment, then nodded. "Yes, please." He stood, still easily, and actually, his back felt better now, and went and fetched another button shirt, a green one that Mama had always liked, with short sleeves, this time.

"Naw, not that one," May said. "You're gonna wear that one when Nurse Julie comes to pick you up. Get me another one."

Franklin should have known May would only hold off on her teasing for a while. "I don't have many," he said, coming back with an embarrassing red, white, and gold Hawaiian shirt that Darryl had gotten him as a joke for Christmas one year.

"Well, now that I know this is your style, I'll just pick you up some," May said as she helped him into it.

"May," Franklin said warningly.

"What? I can't help it. Want you to look good, Cuz," she said. "Now, there's pot roast in the fridge, some meatloaf, seven-layer salad, and a bucket of coleslaw."

"What?" Franklin asked. May hadn't cooked all that while he'd been asleep, had she?

May shrugged. "People always bring food to a funeral. Darryl went and raided Ma's kitchen for you."

"Thank you," Franklin said. He blamed the pain, the medication, and everything else for the way his eyes suddenly pricked.

"I'd give you a hug, but I don't want to hurt you none," May said. "Now, what did I say you should do?"

"Wear the green shirt when Miss Julie comes calling," Franklin told her with a grin.

May expertly *thwacked* him on an undamaged part of his arm. "Not that."

"Rest."

"I mean it. Or I *will* come over and sit on you until you do."

"I will," Franklin said. He wasn't sure he'd be up for much of anything anyway.

"You gonna be okay on your own?" May asked as they neared the door.

A light caught the corner of Franklin's eye. Mama was back, sitting at the kitchen table. She seemed to be whole again, looking like she'd never left.

"Yeah, I'll be fine," Franklin told May with relief.

THOUGH NIGHT WAS FAST APPROACHING, Franklin still went out into his rows of corn behind the house. He wasn't far enough outside of town that he got a full view of the stars, but he could still see a few

LEAH R CUTTER

shining in the deep purple sky. A car swished by on the road going into town, then everything settled down. Franklin breathed in the quiet.

He didn't ever want to leave this place. It was home to him, as comforting as that good pot roast in his fridge, as filling as that side of mashed potatoes he'd had with it. How was he gonna pay the taxes this year? The hospital stay had just taken another chunk of his savings, and he wasn't going to be able to work for a day, maybe two.

His cousins didn't have any cash, and he couldn't ask Aunt Jasmine for money, either, even if Lexine might have a nice insurance payment coming. He'd just have to figure it out, and either win that Kentucky State Fair blue ribbon, or maybe take a second job.

Franklin mourned the three fallen stalks, the leaves already wilting, the corn almost, but not quite ripe yet. The stalks had just been pushed over, not twisted, so he figured it had been either Gloria or Sweet Bess, or heaven help him, yet another ghost. He reached down and picked up one of the fallen soldiers, grunting with pain. He was weak as a kitten, but he still dragged it away to the compost heap, then did the same with the other, panting and sweating by the time he'd finished that simple task.

One side of the fence around the heap had been knocked down, and something had been rooting around. Since they'd been going after food scraps, Franklin figured it were something real, not ghostly. There were plenty of critters around—coons, rabbits, deer, wild dogs, and cats—could have been anything.

Franklin reached down to pick the fence up and stopped as soon as he felt the weight of it. The stalks had been light enough. With his back as it was, though, he shouldn't lift the fence. Normally, he wouldn't have even noticed it. May really would sit on him, or worse, if he tore his stitches.

Frustrated, Franklin let the fence lay where it was, with the stalks on top of the heap, forming a green X.

Back inside, Gloria had joined Mama at the table. Franklin poured himself a glass of sweet tea and sat down at the table with them. He kept the lights down and stayed on the edge of his seat, unable to lean back.

"You okay, Mama?" Franklin asked, getting a glare in return. He looked at her arms, but didn't see any scars—they seemed smooth and all filled out, though the creature had gouged them but good.

"You seem better," Franklin said. "How about you, Miss Gloria? You had a run-in yet with that creature? How is it connected to you, and to Karl?"

Gloria tapped her bright nails on the table, an almost soothing sound, except for the source.

The creature had been in Karl's fields, Franklin was sure of it. It hadn't attacked Karl, though, when he'd shot it, but had come here, to Franklin's house, instead. So did that mean that Karl wasn't special? The thing hadn't attacked Ray, but had just focused on Adrianna.

"What's so special about Karl's fields, then?" Franklin asked Gloria. "What's that thing want with them? Is that why you wanted me to steal Karl's corn, so the creature wouldn't get it?"

Franklin didn't get a response. He hadn't expected one, not really.

There was something there, though, he was sure of it.

However, Karl would never invite Franklin to come and tour his fields.

And going on his own was sure to get his backside full of rock salt.

Franklin was still gonna have to try.

MORNING WAS HARD, harder than even when Franklin's alarm went off too damn early. He wasn't sure he could move, and when he did, he wasn't sure he wanted to keep going. Everything hurt. When Franklin sat up on his narrow bed, the pain took his breath away, and he had to just sit for a moment before turning and sliding his feet onto the ground.

Damn it. Maybe once he got going, it'd be okay.

Franklin gave himself a sponge bath, knowing a real bath or a shower was out of the question for a few more days. It felt good to wash off all the sweat from the day before. He looked at his face in the mirror: Though his dark skin camouflaged the black bags under his eyes, if he looked closely, he could see them. The whites were bloodshot as well. It looked like he was coming off a three-day bender.

The joke about the other guy wasn't funny anymore.

Franklin gingerly made his way to the kitchen, where just Mama sat. "Morning, Mama," Franklin said as he opened the fridge. Maybe breakfast today would just be leftovers. He couldn't see cooking anything. He pulled out the coleslaw, carrying it with both hands to the counter, then reached up for a bowl without thinking. "Ouch!" Damn, he was sore.

Worry spilled out into the room.

Franklin looked around, only to see Mama staring straight at him.

"Mama, I'm fine," Franklin assured her.

It didn't help. Mama was worried about him, worried about her boy.

Was that why she was here, haunting him? Because of that worry?

Mama had always joked about seeing whatever future people paid her to see in her cards. She'd never do it for real, or open up a shop and put up one of those neon signs that said *Psychic—your future read here!*

But she'd had some kind of gift. Franklin was sure of it.

"Mama, did you see something? In your cards? About me and the future?"

Mama nodded her head slowly.

A spike of excitement rushed through Franklin. Mama was responding! Maybe she wouldn't haunt him until he died. "Was it to do with this creature? This spirit that's been haunting me, that broke all those dishes?"

Again, Mama nodded.

"Do you know how to stop it?" Franklin eagerly asked.

The sorrow in the room tripled as Mama shook her head *No*.

Franklin settled himself in the living room for the day, cranking up the old air conditioning unit sticking out of the window, blowing it on him as the heat built up. There wasn't much to see on TV, but Franklin couldn't pay that much attention to it anyway, still sleepy from the medicine and the pain. He propped himself up with pillows on the old green couch and flipped from one old movie to repeats of cop shows and around.

Darryl came by after dinner. He still wore the uniform of the car repair shop he worked at, but his hands had been scrubbed clean.

"Your back ain't too gross, is it?" Darryl asked as Franklin sat down on the closed bathroom commode again.

"May didn't seem bothered," Franklin said.

Darryl snorted. "Not much bothers that girl." He tugged the tape off Franklin's back, not as gentle as May had been. "Eh. I seen worse," was Darryl's only comment. He didn't move as quickly or efficiently as May, and Franklin came to appreciate the training his other cousin had had.

"Did I tell you why I think the thing came after me?" Franklin asked.

"Yeah, that Karl had filled it full of rock salt," Darryl said as he finished Franklin's back and started working on his arms.

The swelling had gone down around the stitches since yesterday, Franklin noticed. Maybe he was getting better.

"You said before that it was going after your lard, and that ghosts like things that were salty," Darryl said. "And you said that whatever it grabbed you with, those whips, were infected."

"According to the doctors, yeah," Franklin said, not liking where the conversation was going.

"So let's poison it," Darryl suggested. "Put up a salt lick near Lexine's cabin, only spike it with antibiotics."

"Where would we get enough antibiotics to kill it?" Franklin asked.

"Well, you'll be seeing that nurse—"

"No," Franklin said. "Absolutely not."

Darryl grinned at him. "Just jossing. They make antibiotic gels and things, right? We can just get some of those, douse the lick good."

Franklin nodded. It might work. But he had his doubts. "Preacher Sinclair wants to go after the thing too."

"That's only because Ma tore a strip off him," Darryl said. "He don't believe in ghosts and spirits and things."

Franklin held his tongue and didn't point out that Darryl had only recently admitted to believing in them as well.

"That don't make sense. He's a reverend," Franklin protested as Darryl helped him back on with his shirt. "Doesn't he believe in things he can't see? I mean, isn't that part of his job description?"

Darryl laughed. "You'd think. But the preacher ain't a bad man."

"So should we take him with us? The next time we go out?" Franklin asked.

"Sounds like a plan," Darryl said with a grin. "I'll arrange it with the reverend. How about tomorrow night? Friday?"

"Well, I ain't going dancing," Franklin pointed out. "And I'm not up for too much. But yeah, let's go put a salt lick out by Lexine's cabin. Sit in your truck and see what we catch."

~

FRANKLIN WASN'T EXPECTING any more visitors, so he'd taken off his shirt and just let the cool breeze from the AC in the living room window blow on his bare skin. He hadn't turned on any lights, either, just let the glow from the TV light the room. Mama was back in the kitchen, this time with Gloria, who were both acting mad again. Franklin didn't know at what.

When someone knocked loudly at the front door, Franklin debated not getting up to see who it was. But ghosts and spirits didn't knock. He didn't do more than kind of drape his shirt over his chest, though.

The red and blue lights flashing in his driveway made Franklin's gut drop through to the bottoms of his bare feet.

"There's been another attack," the sheriff said abruptly, without even saying hello.

"Who?" Franklin asked, slipping one of his sleeves on.

"Darryl."

THE CREATURE HAD FOUND Darryl and attacked him while he was driving his truck up the highway. Fortunately, Darryl had steered onto the shoulder before he slammed into anyone, then had gotten himself out of the truck cabin before the thing could do too much damage.

Franklin didn't know why the creature didn't just follow him—seemed his cousin was just lucky that way.

Darryl was still all torn to hell. The creature had wrapped its thorn whips around his forearms and sliced them up, where they'd been clutching the steering wheel.

Sheriff Thompson brought Franklin to the hospital. Darryl was still in admitting—they weren't going to have to do much but give him some stitches. Since they'd recognized the wounds from when Franklin came in, they'd set Darryl up on antibiotics right away. He sat on what looked like a dentist's chair, with a doctor in a white coat sitting beside him.

"Don't know what you boys been hunting," the doctor said as he stitched away at Darryl's arm. "But it sure got some claws."

Neither Franklin, Darryl, nor the sheriff said anything.

"Why didn't it come after you after you'd thrown yourself from the truck?" Franklin asked when the doctor had gone.

"'Cause I'd grabbed my shotgun and winged it," Daryl said with a grin. "But that rock salt didn't really stop it."

Franklin nodded, glad that the thing hadn't come after him again in retaliation. Hopefully it hadn't gone after anyone else, either.

"I don't like it," the sheriff said sourly. "I still don't know what it was that attacked you two, or Lexine, or Earl Jackson."

Franklin didn't point out that he'd already told the sheriff what it was. It was just that the sheriff didn't want to believe it.

"Still," the sheriff said. "I hate to admit it. But. Something's out there. And it's my duty to stop it. Before it kills someone else."

"We're gonna try to trap it, and poison it," Darryl said eagerly. "Get a salt lick, lace it with antibiotic cream."

The sheriff listened, rubbing his forefinger and thumb over his long mustache and around his mouth, nodding his head.

"Do you think that'll work?" the sheriff asked Franklin.

"Beats me, sir," Franklin said. "I'm just about run out of ideas how to kill it." If Mama, who could maybe see the future and was already a ghost, didn't know how, he wasn't sure he could figure it out.

"Let me know how your experiment goes," Sheriff Thompson finally said. "But you get out of there if that thing turns on you. I do *not* want to bring your mother any more bad news. You hear me?"

"Yes, sir," Franklin said.

Darryl just grinned. "It ain't gonna get us. It ain't got either of us yet."

"'Yet' is kind of the operative word there, don't you think?" the sheriff asked as he walked off.

Darryl dropped his smile after the sheriff had gone. "That creature's real dangerous," he told Franklin seriously. "And now, not only has it come after you, it's come after me. We're gonna get it. We're gonna send it back to Hell where it belongs."

Franklin just hoped they didn't end up dying in the process.

CHAPTER 9

FRANKLIN SPENT MOST OF FRIDAY relaxing again. May wouldn't be by until later that night to change the dressing on his back. He took off the bandages on his arms himself, and then wrapped them back up with a much lighter gauze. He could start leaving the bandages off at night, letting 'em air, starting Saturday. Then he returned to his pile of pillows on the couch and his TV, flipping through the channels during the commercials.

When his phone rang about 4 PM, he expected it to be Darryl with more of his plans.

It was Ray Sorrel, instead. "So how'd you like some visitors?" Ray asked.

"Are you sure?" Franklin said in return. He knew they'd been camping out for some time now, under the tree men, so Adrianna would be safe.

"It's Adrianna actually, who's insisting. She thinks that since the creature's already attacked you, it won't go back there. That you drove it off, like she did."

"It wasn't really me who drove it off. I just…got away. Plus, it's attacked my cousin Darryl, in his truck."

"Is he all right?"

"Shook up. Gouged. But yeah, he's fine."

"We're coming anyway," Ray said firmly. "Can't live our lives afraid of shadows, or always outdoors. Besides," Ray paused, then lowered his voice. "Adrianna says she wants to try picking up power lines in other places now. She swears it'll protect you. If she can do it at all."

"Come on by, then," Franklin told him. After he hung up, he made more tea and set up for a picnic outside, in the back.

Ray and Adrianna knocked on the door soon after that.

"It's so good to see you," Adrianna said, taking Franklin's hand at the door but not coming inside. She wore one of her usual flowy dresses, in yellows and oranges that made her skin seem more pale and her features more fragile, like she was turning into a porcelain doll.

"Glad you're on your feet," Ray said.

"I planned on having tea out back," Franklin told them. He didn't want Adrianna to refuse to come inside—Mama might get angry at that.

"Anything I can help with?" Ray asked, edging across the threshold.

"Sure. Let me show Miss Adrianna the table first," Franklin said.

They walked around the edge of the house, to the white tables and chairs in the back, looking out toward his rows of corn. The Kentucky bluegrass Franklin had growing out there was lush and green. Franklin was gonna have to cut it again, soon. It felt peaceful out there, even in the heat of the day, with the loud crickets and cicadas.

"I'll be right back," Franklin assured her.

"Take your time, dear," Adrianna said. She didn't sit, but stayed standing, staring out at the fields.

Franklin didn't trust whatever she'd get up to, so he hurried into the house.

"How's she doing?" Franklin asked Ray as he put the pitcher of iced tea and three glasses on a tray that already held the last of the cookies that May had brought over from the funeral.

"She's getting stranger," Ray admitted. "I'm afraid I'm losing her. She barely talks with me anymore."

"I'm sorry, Ray," Franklin said. He wasn't sure what advice to offer the older man, if there was anything he could say that would help. "Just keep letting her know she's your lady," he finally came up with. "She'll come back."

Ray gave a bitter laugh. "That's what the songs say, don't they? But I don't know if that'll be true for us."

"It's only been a couple of days," Franklin pointed out.

"No, this has been coming for a while. Like the thing with the koi pond," Ray said. "That wasn't the start of it." He sighed. "We should get out there."

Franklin let Ray carry the tray, both to give him something to do, as well as to not put any strain on his arms or back. Adrianna was sitting by now. She scolded them, saying, "I didn't know what you two had gotten into, making me wait so long."

"I'm sorry, dear," Ray said, leaning over and kissing her forehead.

They stayed like that for a second, Adrianna leaning into Ray, something deep and precious passing between them.

Maybe Ray had been wrong about Adrianna pulling away.

After Franklin served the tea, Adrianna asked, "Could you tell me what happened the night you were attacked, dear?"

Franklin started off with explaining about Sweet Bess, going in through the root cellar, how the thing had tore up his kitchen, and how Mama had stepped in so he could get away.

"It's those things we love, or who love us, that are the most effective against this creature, aren't they?" Adrianna mused.

"Huh. That's what Billy said," Franklin replied. "He said it was pure evil, and the only way to fight it was with love."

"He may have been onto something," Ray said.

"What, we're supposed to hug it to death?" Franklin asked, repeating Darryl's question.

"No, dear," Adrianna said. "Turn the other cheek is often wrongly used. You have to *fight* it using love, with the things you love."

"What do you mean?" Franklin asked. He'd never thought about fighting using love before.

"Now, I know Ray has been questioning whether I still love him or not," Adrianna said slyly.

"Dear—" Ray started.

"Let me finish. I do love you, Ray. But I can't use you to fight. I have to use the other things I love, if I want to protect you," Adrianna said clearly, though her eyes were starting to haze over.

"You don't have to fight anything," Franklin said as Adrianna turned her gaze from them and out over the fields.

"But I must," Adrianna said in a voice that was no longer her own: It had grown dark and husky, like a clouded night.

Franklin shivered. The grace that had taken over Darryl hadn't been frightening. It had been more like he'd finally stepped into his real skin.

With Adrianna, it was like something else had stepped inside her.

Adrianna rose sluggishly and walked—like she was sleepwalking —to the edge of the corn rows, where she raised her hands with her fingers spread wide, then lowered them toward the ground.

Even in the afternoon light, Franklin saw the trails starting, glowing white, flowing from her fingers and spreading out across the land, like painted white stripes.

"What's she doing, Ray?" Franklin asked, alarmed. He went to stand behind Adrianna. All the hair along the back of his neck stood up and chills ran down his spine, like a platoon of ghosts stood breathing over his shoulder.

"I don't know," Ray said, standing behind him. "What'cha doing, honey?"

Adrianna didn't bother to reply. Slowly, she turned her hands and curled her fingers around, grasping the lines like they were thick cables. The muscles in her bare arms strained as she raised her hands up. She flicked her wrists once, sending the lines cascading down, like reins on a set of horses.

A sizzling noise filled the air, like a bad electronic transformer, the pitch winding up until the sound hurt Franklin's ears. What the hell was she doing? What kind of power had she raised?

Adrianna flicked her wrists again. The power surged along the lines, bouncing from the end, up to Adrianna, and back again. She shivered and sweat broke out along her forehead.

Was she strong enough to maintain these lines? Or was she gonna collapse any moment now?

Suddenly, the creature appeared. It stayed in the distance, at the edge of Franklin's property. Fear held Franklin to the spot. What the hell was he going to do if it attacked again? How could he protect not just himself, but Adrianna?

Adrianna whipped one of the power lines in her left hand toward the thing, flailing it open, as if striking it with a barbed whip.

How could she do that? Franklin hadn't thought that someone as soft and flaky as Adrianna would even have it in her to fight.

Fury poured from the creature. *How dare its prey attack?* It whirled faster, then hopped up, on top of the line of power emanating from Adrianna.

Adrianna flicked her wrists again, trying to toss the creature off, but it held on tenaciously.

Then it started riding the line back.

It was coming to attack.

Adrianna pulled with her right hand, trying to bring those lines up high enough to reach the creature. But she couldn't pull hard enough, or move fast enough.

The thing's long whips were at the ready, the stingers stretched out, eager to hurt and maim.

"Let go!" Franklin cried. "Let it fall!" That was the only way he could get both of them out of there.

With a hoarse shout, Adrianna raised her power lines one last time, up above her head, then brought them down, past her knees.

It wasn't enough to knock the creature loose.

Adrianna flung her hands wide open, dropping the lines. She staggered back, and only Ray catching her prevented her from falling.

The creature stayed balanced for a moment, then it fell to the ground as the lines fell back.

Then the line it was on turned black, and the spirit raced away from them, following the black line, slurping up all the power that had been raised.

Shit. Was that thing getting stronger now? It looked bigger. But at least it was heading away from them.

Franklin turned back toward Adrianna. She rested against Ray, his hands under her elbows, helping her stand. Her eyes were clear again, but half-mast, and her pale face now looked sickly.

Franklin looked back out, over his field. The creature was at least twice the size it had been, before it disappeared off the edge of the property.

What had they done?

~

FRANKLIN STOOD BY, helpless as Ray bundled Adrianna back into their car. He wanted to help, but just the appearance of the creature had set all his wounds throbbing: He couldn't risk trying to help pick Adrianna up, then dropping her or pulling out his stitches or something.

"I'm sorry, Franklin," Ray said, coming over to stand next to him in the driveway of the house. "Feeding that thing, making it stronger, was the farthest thing from what Adrianna wanted to do."

"I know," Franklin said. But that's just what they'd done. They'd made it stronger, more deadly. Who would it attack next? Who would it kill?

"I wanted to let you know something else," Ray said. "I'd meant to tell you earlier, but…anyway. Earl? Hadn't just gone to Lexine's place. He'd also been looking at the deed to Karl Metzger's farm."

"Was he looking to buy it?" Franklin asked, puzzled. Karl's place was far too close to town for a resort. Maybe Earl had just wanted to talk to Karl about his crops, since they were the best in the county.

"I've asked his office, but no one knows for certain," Ray said.

"Thanks," Franklin said. He was gonna have to pay Karl another visit, and he wasn't looking forward to that.

A short while after Franklin finished dinner, May came knocking on the door, with Darryl on her heels. "No, he's not going out with you, not anywhere," she argued as they walked in.

"But I think we can damage this thing, maybe kill it," Darryl said.

"Y'all are more likely to get yourselves killed," May said. She took one look at Franklin. "Get over here, into the light," she ordered.

Sheepishly, Franklin moved into the light in the kitchen.

"What the hell did you do to yourself?" May asked. "You forget your antibiotics?"

Franklin shook his head, then explained how Adrianna had been trying to help but had ended up feeding the creature instead.

"So it's stronger now, than it was?" May asked. "And you two fools think you're gonna stop it with a little salt lick?"

A knock came at the door.

"Lord help me. Three fools?" May asked when she saw Preacher Sinclair standing on the porch.

"I beg your pardon?" the preacher asked, his tone chilly.

"Never mind," May said. "I need to change this one's bandages, and then y'all can go barreling into Hell as far as I'm concerned. Come on." She stalked out of the room.

"There's some tea, reverend," Franklin said. "I'll be right back." He squeezed past May in the tiny bathroom, sitting down on the closed commode.

May closed the door. "What the hell do you think you're doing, getting the preacher involved?" she whispered urgently.

"The thing's evil," Franklin whispered back. "Like a demon. Maybe the preacher can help."

"You think prayers are gonna stop what did this to you?" May asked, raising up Franklin's arm, showing him the puffed-up stitches.

"The power lines that Adrianna raised could have been from God," Franklin said stubbornly. "They sure as hell weren't human."

May shook her head and angrily yanked the tape off Franklin's back.

"Ow!" he complained.

"You're gonna hurt so much worse before the night's out," May warned darkly. "Take my word."

She wouldn't say anything else as she quickly bandaged him back up, admonishing him not to forget his pills before she marched right back out the front door.

"I take it she doesn't approve of this venture," Preacher Sinclair said.

"No sir, she don't," Darryl replied.

"I'll talk with her Sunday," the preacher said. He paused, took a deep breath, clasped his hands in front of him, and started in. "I prayed long and hard before coming to this decision. It was as though God was showing me a clear path, a new direction," the preacher said, gaining steam. "Lord, I asked him, where should I go? Has the devil taken form here, on earth? And the Lord said, Son—'cause he always calls me son—Son, you should go. You should believe. You need to truly know evil before you can do good." The preacher put one hand up in the air and the other over his heart. "I swear the Word had never been so clear."

Franklin didn't know what to believe. Had the preacher really been speaking to God? Or was it just for show, like his sermons where he got so riled up?

"That's great, reverend," Darryl said dryly. "But we should get going. Bring your lard," he added to Franklin as he walked out.

"Lead the way," the preacher said. "I am your humble follower in this pursuit."

Franklin shook his head as he picked up the jar of lard and locked the door. May might have been right. They was all gonna hurt before the night was out.

Darryl proudly lowered the back of the truck bed, showing the two-foot-square cube of salt he had back there. It oozed with antibiotic cream. "Spread it on top, thick," Darryl directed, handing Franklin a plastic knife.

Franklin dipped into lard with a sigh, then dripped it onto the top of the salt lick. He hated wasting good lard this way. Maybe he should have just gotten some bacon grease or something instead.

Hopefully, though, the creature would like it enough that it might also lick up the antibiotic cream, and do some damage to itself.

They all jammed together into the front of Darryl's truck, Franklin in the middle, boxed in by Darryl and the preacher. "We going out to Lexine's cabin?" Franklin asked as Darryl peeled out of the driveway, jostling Franklin's back and causing pain to shoot up his spine.

"That way, yeah," Darryl said. "So we got the salt lick, and we've covered it with stuff we hope is poisonous to the creature. What you got, reverend?"

"The power of prayer," Preacher Sinclair said sincerely. "If that thing is as evil as y'all claim, it should falter when faced with the Word of God."

Franklin shook his head but didn't say anything. He wanted to believe the reverend. He did.

He was afraid, though, that they were all heading straight for disaster.

~

THE WOODS HID ALL the light from the sky, tripling the dark. Franklin didn't like how closed in they felt. He didn't see Sweet Bess, but he could swear he heard her snorting, somewhere close.

Darryl had placed the lick out on the road, in the beams of the headlights from the truck. They sat, the three of them, sweating in the cab of the truck, waiting for something to happen.

"Did you hear the one about—" Darryl started.

Franklin *thwapped* him on the thigh.

"What? It was clean. Mostly," Darryl said, unrepentant.

"You may not believe it, but I was a young man myself, once," Preacher Sinclair said. "I remember those jokes, and that time when flesh was the only thing on my mind."

Franklin shifted in his seat, uncomfortable. He didn't want to hear about anyone's experience with the flesh.

"But my time with the Lord has been just as sweet, and fulfilling," the preacher went on.

"Ma's wondered why you ain't married," Darryl said.

The preacher shook his head. "I was, a long time ago. Lost her after a long hard fight to cancer." Preacher Sinclair paused. "I never found the heart in me to give it away again."

"We're sorry for your loss," Franklin said automatically.

"It was a long time ago. I know she's in a better place. I found comfort in the Lord," the preacher said. "I joined His ministry soon after. I needed saving after what I'd done. How I'd failed her."

Franklin nodded. That made sense to him, though the reverend probably shouldn't beat himself up that way.

"Is that something moving?" Darryl asked, peering out the windshield.

The wind picked up suddenly, pushing the branches around, sending the leaves dancing through the glow of the headlights. All the hair on the back of Franklin's neck pricked up.

"I think we got company," Franklin said softly. A chill passed through him, making him shiver in the humid cab.

The other two looked at him. "Really?" Darryl asked, curious.

"Can't you feel that?" Franklin asked, the wounds on his arms starting to throb.

"Feel what?" the preacher asked.

"That," Franklin said, pointing straight ahead.

The thing appeared in front of the truck, its gray dust-devil center sparkling with the power Adrianna had fed it that afternoon. It had gained size, too: Instead of being about the size of a fat twelve-year-old boy, now it was more like the size of an ox.

"I don't see anything," the preacher said.

"Me neither," Darryl said.

Shit. How could Franklin show them this creature? "It's taller, now," Franklin said softly. "It's bumping up against the salt lick. It has these long whips, at least a dozen of 'em, wrapped tightly around its body. It looks like a sickness, a gray tornado of misery."

"Why can't I see it?" Darryl complained.

"Your arms don't ache?" Franklin asked.

"Nope," Darryl said, shaking his head. "Yours do?"

Franklin nodded his head. When Lexine had wanted to share her visitors, she'd reached out her hand to Franklin. Maybe he could do the same....

"Take my hand," Franklin said in desperation. "Maybe you'll see more if we're touching."

The preacher said, "I'm not sure that's a good idea."

Darryl glanced over at the reverend, then took Franklin's offered hand.

The grip around Franklin's fingers tightened to the point of pain. "I see...something," Darryl said. "Like a wispy cloud."

"It's more than that. Bigger," Franklin said.

With a sigh, the preacher took Franklin's other hand. He gasped, then he said sternly, "There's nothing there. What I'm seeing is just the power of suggestion. It's fog, rolled in from the trees, reflected in your headlights." But he didn't let go of Franklin's hand. And he did start praying in earnest: "Lord, I need your protection this dark night. Here in the shadow of things, defend me from the evil before me."

"That's not just fog, is it?" Darryl asked.

Franklin shook his head. Sweat poured down his sides and his skin grew clammy. His wounds all ached. The darkness pressed in harder, like it was trying to flatten him back, push him away from the light in the world.

The thing hadn't seemed to notice them. It was focused on the salt lick, brushing up against it like a cat, focused on the top, where Franklin had put the lard of Sweet Bess.

"I think it's working," Franklin said softly. The thing was shrinking! It whirled faster, but tighter, the white sparks from Adrianna's power lines dying. "It's getting sick," he added. It wobbled, now, as it spun, sliding to one side, then the other, and finally, out of the headlights.

"Did it just disappear?" Darryl asked.

"Uh huh," Franklin said. He wasn't about to leave the truck to see if it had actually fallen down.

"Woo hoo!" Darryl hooted, banging his free hand on the steering wheel. "We did it!"

"Maybe," Franklin said. "Let's wait."

"We should go after it," the preacher said. "Continue to expose it to the Word of God."

"I don't think—" Franklin said. He jumped in his seat when the thing suddenly came roaring back.

Wind slammed into the side of the truck. Leaves, branches, and dirt hit the windshield. The thing whipped out at the salt lick, tearing it apart. Lines of salt went flying through the air.

"Tell me you at least saw that," Franklin said. He wished he could get farther away, but he couldn't press his back hard against the seat.

"Something's attacking the salt lick," Darryl said. "Like a storm cloud, or something."

Franklin knew the moment the creature spotted them.

"Go," Franklin told Darryl. "GO!"

Darryl let go of Franklin's hand, but the preacher held on, praying for all he was worth. "LORD! You must save this sinner! Turn back the evil, send the darkness back to where it belongs."

The truck rumbled to life. Darryl threw it into reverse. "Hang on!" Darryl said as he threw his arm over the seat and looked behind.

The thing raced after them, whirling mad. It might have been diminished, but its fury was greater than ever.

It gained on them.

"Faster!" Franklin cried. Every bump they took jarred his back, but he didn't care.

That thing could kill the three of them out here in the woods, and no one would find them for days.

Darryl glanced out the front, then floored it. They skidded along the gravel. Bushes scratched the sides of the truck.

Preacher Sinclair continued praying out loud. "Please, Lord, let the evil before me pass," he pleaded. "Shelter me from the darkness."

Franklin wondered what the man saw. The creature's *intent* spilled out into the cab of the truck: It wanted all of them maimed, hurt, dead. How dare they attack it? How dare they hurt it? They were puny and it would kill all of them, as painfully as it could.

"Can't you turn this thing around?" Franklin asked as Darryl swore and slowed down.

Darryl slammed on the brakes. "Fuck it," he said through gritted teeth. He threw the truck into forward and gunned it.

"I'm gonna run down that fucker," Darryl said, heading straight for it.

The creature stopped, but didn't seem worried. It snapped its whip arms, as if waiting, daring them to come, like some demented game of chicken.

"This is stupid, Darryl!" Franklin said, as he put his arm on the dashboard and braced for the impact.

"I'm tired of this thing," Darryl said.

Then they collided.

The creature didn't bounce away, or even push back. Instead, it pushed *through* the truck, passing into the bumper, the engine, and into the cab itself.

And then straight through Franklin.

CHAPTER 10

FRANKLIN HAD NEVER FELT SUCH cold in all his life, not even that time it'd snowed and Darryl had stuck a handful of it down the front of Franklin's jeans.

He tried to breathe through his frozen lungs, but it was like breathing under water. Ice crystals formed along his throat, making it feel like what little air coming through was going across the tips of knives. Everything had a blue haze to it: the dashboard of the truck, the woods outside, even his own hands, up to his blue-tinged fingernails. Preacher Sinclair was saying something—yelling, even—but the ice had plugged Franklin's ears. A blue halo shone around the preacher's afro. Maybe someday, Franklin could ask Mama to do something like that for him.

Just as suddenly, the world roared back in, the frozen moment passed. But Franklin was still cold, still chilled, still shook even though every cut and scrape and gouge throbbed with pain. "Home," Franklin said, his teeth chattering.

"What the hell happened?" the preacher demanded. "That thing —is it inside of you now, son?" He wrapped his hands around Franklin's head. "You can be healed. All we have to do is pray. God, save this child. Bring your mercy down—"

"Preacher," Franklin pleaded, trying to shake his head free. "Stop it!"

Darryl got them out of the woods and pulled over on the highway. He stopped the truck and leapt out of it.

Damn it. Darryl couldn't leave. Franklin couldn't fight both the preacher and the effects of the thing.

The preacher continued praying, with his warm hands pressed against Franklin's still frozen chest. "We can exorcise this thing," the preacher continued. "Pray it right out of you."

Darryl hopped back into the cab after just a moment, a silver emergency blanket in his hands. "Stop trying to save his soul and actually help him," Darryl instructed the preacher, handing him one end of the blanket.

Franklin shivered, helpless, as they wrapped the blanket around him.

"It's the ice of Hell, isn't it," Preacher Sinclair said.

"This what you was afraid of? With Sweet Bess?" Darryl asked, ignoring the preacher, getting the blanket tucked in around Franklin, then starting up the truck again. He blasted the heat, directing the vents at Franklin.

Franklin could barely feel the breeze they made, let alone the warmth. "Yes," he managed to say. "Only worse." So much worse. Everything felt displaced inside of him. He was breathing a bit better, but it still hurt. *Jesus*, everything hurt. He only knew where his arms and legs were because of the pain, but he didn't think he could even stand.

"I'm sorry," Darryl said quietly.

"I am too," the preacher said. "We should go to the church. So I can drive the demon out of him."

"The demon's not in him," Darryl said.

"Are you sure?" Preacher Sinclair asked. "It passed into the truck, into *him*, then disappeared. It didn't pass out of the truck."

"That thing inside you?" Darryl asked Franklin.

"No," Franklin said, shaking his head. *Ow.* That had been a mistake. He tried not to move, though he winced at every bump Darryl took at high speed.

"Are you certain, son?" the preacher asked.

"Yes," Franklin said. "You couldn't see it because I passed out, and I couldn't see it anymore."

"If you say so," Preacher Sinclair said. But he still watched Franklin warily, as if expecting the creature to pop out of his chest at any time, like some kind of alien.

~

"How long will this last?" Darryl asked as he helped Franklin up the stairs to his house. The kitchen was quiet and empty.

Where the hell was Mama? That thing hadn't come here and attacked her again, had it?

"Day, maybe two," Franklin said as he staggered on his own to one of the kitchen chairs then collapsed down into it. He was getting better, but he knew it would take a while for all the effects to disappear.

That thing had passed through the core of him. Franklin still felt hollowed out.

"I'm sorry," Darryl said again.

"Don't be," Franklin said firmly. "Much better that it pass through me. Couldn't have it get inside the truck and attack the three of us, you know?"

Darryl nodded. He helped himself to one of Franklin's beers, or rather, the beers in Franklin's fridge that Darryl had put there. "Preacher still thinks you're possessed."

Franklin nodded wearily. "Took us long enough to get him to believe. Now he's seeing evil everywhere."

Darryl chuckled. "All you gotta do is let him baptize you again. Then he'll think you're clean. Probably."

Franklin shivered at the thought. He wasn't going to Wolf River and be baptized in the waters tonight, that was for damn sure. "Maybe this weekend," Franklin said. The preacher had been awfully worried. "I need to sleep. That'll help this thing pass."

"That's right. You got that big date tomorrow, don't you?" Darryl teased.

Franklin glared at Darryl. "I'm too tired to argue with you. But I'm not going just to see Julie. Maybe Lexine talked with these folks, talked about her property, or about that Earl Jackson."

"You're smarter than you look," Darryl said.

"So are you. That idea with the salt lick was a good one. But I don't think the creature will fall for it twice," Franklin said.

Darryl nodded. "We'll figure something out."

"We'd better," Franklin said. "'Cause it's got a taste of our blood. And it wants more."

FRANKLIN'S FRUSTRATION near boiled over by 10 AM. He couldn't lift anything—the attack from the night before had left him weak and in pain. Even trying to get dishes out of the fridge left him trembling. His field had lost another stalk of corn, but he couldn't drag the fallen combatant to the compost heap. He couldn't do laundry, or change the bandages on his back. Everything felt too closed in, like he was wrapped in scratchy blankets and couldn't get out.

Sick and tired of being sick and tired, Franklin threw himself back on the couch, among his piles of pillows, watching one bad movie after another. He'd tried to watch the science fiction channel, but the ghosts and demons not only looked fake, they didn't behave like any he knew.

Mama hadn't reappeared. Neither had Gloria.

Was Franklin just too tired and beat up to see them? Or did the hollowed-out feeling he'd had since the creature passed through him mean something? Had he actually been scooped out?

Had the creature, somehow, taken his ability to see ghosts?

If that was the case, Franklin didn't know whether to be happy or sad. Not having Mama or anyone else haunting him, making him special and weird and different, that might be a relief.

Maybe it meant the creature couldn't attack him again. He was safe.

But Franklin also would miss the wonder of the other world. He didn't just want to have to take the existence of spirits on *faith* alone.

He wanted to do more than just believe. Plus, this had always been his duty. He didn't know if it was his calling, like how the Lord had called the preacher into his ministry. But it didn't feel right, not seeing Mama around.

If the creature had taken Franklin's ability, how could he get it back? He didn't want to pass through that thing again. Even if he did, there wasn't any guarantee that he'd get his power back, and that the creature wouldn't take something more, something bigger or more important.

Later that afternoon, Franklin changed the bandages on his arms. The swelling had started going back down, and the skin didn't feel so hot to him, like a fever lived just underneath the scars. He still covered them back up. It didn't feel right, going to meet a bunch of strangers with all his sores exposed.

"Brought you some more food," May called as she let herself in the door around suppertime.

"Are people still bringing stuff to Aunt Jasmine's?" Franklin asked.

"Darling, she's got a freezer full at this point," May replied. "She can afford to share more than this."

"I'll go see her tomorrow, after church," Franklin said. "How's she holding up?"

"You know Ma. Tougher than nails." May hesitated, then continued. "She's still lost weight. And there's a sadness, deep and still, that comes up." May sighed. "I miss Lexine too," she said quietly.

"Same here," Franklin said, the pain not just in his back and his arms, but his gut as well. He'd been so busy, he really hadn't been taking any time to mourn.

And he still gotten the thing that had gouged up Lexine, had hurt him, Daryl, Adrianna.

He was out of ideas how to go about it, though.

~

FRANKLIN PUT on the pretty green shirt that May had told him to wear for Julie, as well as a nice pair of light gray pants and sandals.

He was ready at least thirty minutes before Julie said she'd come by. He didn't know what to do with himself as he waited.

Mama still hadn't returned to her place at the kitchen table.

Feeling like he had as a boy when he'd played doorbell-ditch on the neighbors, Franklin walked around the table, pulled out the chair that Mama normally sat in, then slid into it himself.

No chilling effect of a ghostly body walked down his spine, no sense of *other* filled him.

There was nothing there. Nobody but him in the quiet kitchen.

What had happened to Mama? Had she passed on? He doubted it. She still had things to do. Then where was she? Had that creature destroyed her? Or was she settling her account somewhere else?

The minutes ticked by in the empty kitchen, and Franklin prayed for the first time ever that his gift hadn't deserted him.

JULIE RANG the front doorbell right on time. Franklin was up and at the door seconds later, pulling it open.

"Hi," Franklin said. "It's good to see you." She looked just lovely, wearing a sky-blue sleeveless shirt and white shorts-skirt.

"Nice to see you too," Julie said. She stepped into the hallway at Franklin's invitation. "You look better," she added, examining his face critically. "But you haven't been taking it easy, have you?"

"Guilty as charged, ma'am," Franklin admitted. He didn't know how much he could tell Julie about the creature, how much Lexine had told the group about her own abilities.

"It won't be stressful tonight," Julie promised. "And I'll bring you back anytime you want. You just say the word."

"Thank you," Franklin said. He followed Julie out to her car, an old gray Ford Focus.

"It may look like a wreck," Julie apologized. "But it's got great heart."

The interior was a matching gray, the seats clean but stained, and it smelled musty. Franklin eased himself in carefully, trying not to put any pressure on his back.

Julie looked at him. "The shocks aren't great, I'm afraid. You're going to feel every bump, aren't you?"

"It'll be all right," Franklin assured her.

Julie started the car. It gave a deep rumble. "Whatcha got in there?" Franklin asked.

"V-8," Julie said with a grin. "My dad's a mechanic. Taught me all about cars. He took out the puny two-point-oh and put in a powerhouse." She spun gravel under her tires as they climbed out of the driveway and up to the street.

"How many speeding tickets you got?" Franklin teased.

"Too many to count," Julie admitted. "Most of the time I just tell 'em I'm a nurse and I got an emergency to get to."

"Smart," Franklin said. "So how'd you end up doing that? Nursing?"

"Dad wanted me to be a doctor," Julie said. "Pushed me hard. I just don't want that kind of responsibility, you know? I'd rather be the power behind the throne, the one who actually does the work, rather than the king."

"I have a cousin who wanted to be an EMT. She's been changing my bandages for me, on my back. Doing a real good job, too," Franklin said.

Julie laughed and shook her head. "I'd thought about that too, but I'm not that much of an adrenaline junkie. Rather get my kicks speeding down the road, you know?"

Franklin didn't—he didn't want to admit to her that he didn't have a car. The silence grew between them for a few moments—not quite uncomfortable but getting there—before Franklin asked, "Did you grow up around here?"

"Close enough. I grew up in Hendrickson."

"Never heard of it," Franklin admitted.

"It's a wide spot in the road," Julie said. "Nothing much there but farms, cattle, and a few shops. There was no way I was staying. How about you?"

"Born and raised here," Franklin told her. "But mostly it was Mama and me. Papa died when I was two. That's when Mama bought the house, with the insurance money." Franklin had used most of her life insurance money to pay off the rest of the mortgage, so he was free and clear—only had to pay taxes on it.

"Lexine was your cousin, right?" Julie asked.

"Mama's sister, Aunt Jasmine's kid. By marriage. But that didn't matter, not really. We were all one family, all of us raised together. Darryl and May and Jason and Lexine—they was really like brothers and sisters to me."

"What's your favorite memory of Lexine?" Julie asked quietly.

Franklin thought for a moment. He couldn't talk about the spirits Lexine showed him. He'd never forget the one time in the spring when Wolf River had been flooding, and she'd shown him the raging spirit of the water. There were other memories, though, that he had, that were special. "Alpine strawberries grew wild in the fields near her place. You ever have those?"

Julie shook her head.

"They're about the size of a pine nut," Franklin said. "And about that shape, too. But they're sweeter than all get out. And they right near explode with flavor. Like the perfect strawberry." He smiled at the memory. "Lexine brought a handful of those over one night, along with some lemonade blueberries, the ones that are pale pink?"

"Never had those either," Julie said.

"So Lexine brought over a just a handful. I made fun of them, I'll admit. They was so tiny! But she served them up with some flavored ice. We sat out back, overlooking the fields, and just talked while the stars came out." It really was one of his nicer memories, both of them talking about the future, where they'd be in a few years.

"That's lovely," Julie said. "I'll always remember the night Lexine taught me how to make a proper smudging stick."

"A what?" Franklin asked.

"When you want to purify a place, you burn a smudge stick, wave the sacred smoke into the corners and call the gods to sanctify the area," Julie said seriously.

"What gods?" Franklin asked, wary. What had Lexine been getting into with this group?

"Like Bridget, the goddess of hospitality, and Eleanor, the goddess of health. So your house or your room or your sanctuary will be welcoming and open to the right spirits," Julie said seriously.

"Huh," Franklin said. "Do you often work with spirits?" he asked, since Julie seemed to believe in them, at any rate.

"I'm not as sensitive as Lexine was," Julie admitted. "She always knew where the soul of a place was, or what it was feeling."

"That was her gift," Franklin said.

Julie threw him a quick smile. "Yes, yes it was. She said you weren't bad at it, either."

"Spirits was more Lexine's area, not mine," Franklin said cautiously.

They sped through the dark in silence for a bit before Julie asked, "So what is your area? If spirits were Lexine's?"

"You know. This and that," Franklin said, not feeling like he could answer.

"There are folks in town who say you speak to ghosts," Julie said quietly.

"Maybe," Franklin admitted. "Maybe not. I ain't been seeing many recently. Not since I got hurt." He didn't want to tell her about the creature, or how it had affected him.

"That makes sense," Julie said seriously. "It wasn't just your body that was hurt, but your heart, too. The thing that attacked you was trying to suck out your soul."

"Well, it didn't succeed," Franklin told her. He'd see his ghosts again, help them pass along. He'd get back to doing his duty.

He'd see Mama at least one more time.

THE MEETING that night was held in a converted shack in the backyard of another member's house—Eddie, as she introduced herself, an older white woman with tanned, leathery skin, wild white curls, and blue eyes.

"Delighted to meet you," Eddie said as she greeted them at the gate to the yard. "Y'all can just go on back. The space's already been sanctified, blessed by the spirits and the gods."

"Blessed be," Julie said in reply.

"Ah, thanks," Franklin said. He really didn't know what this group was all about. He wasn't ever going to tell Preacher Sinclair about them.

The shack wasn't too big, smaller than a one-car garage. It had the look of an artist's studio, like something Adrianna would pester Ray into building, with red-painted wooden shingles covering the outer walls, white trim, and a gray tiled roof. Sweet incense oozed from it, floating over the wet grass. A large sun, plain-looking, made out of baked reddish pottery, hung on one side of the door, while a matching moon hung on the other side. Pretty white Christmas-tree lights outlined the doorframe.

Dark black curtains covered the door. Julie reached beyond Franklin and held them to one side, gesturing for him to go in first.

Franklin reminded himself that Lexine had trusted this group. He took a deep breath of the clean night air, ducked his head, and walked in.

Inside were almost a dozen men and women, all crowded around the edges of the room. Work benches lined two of the walls, and under the smell of the incense came the metallic scent of shellac and paint. A round table covered with an off-white tablecloth stood in the center of the room. Incense smoked from a flat, black-metal plate. Four white crystals, each the size of Franklin's fist, were spread out like a new-age cross on one side.

In the center of the table lay a knife. The blade wasn't flat, but made up of three points, more like a pick. The handle was black, wrapped in leather, and the iron looked cold and hard. It gave Franklin the willies. There was something to that blade, something not of this world.

Something not entirely good.

What the hell was this group?

Julie came to stand next to him. She introduced him around the room as Lexine's cousin, but Franklin couldn't hold onto any of their names. Finally, Eddie came in, trailing behind one more man. "Let's all get together, one big circle," Eddie directed.

Franklin shuffled to the side. Julie took one hand, and the woman next to him took the other.

Eddie cleared her throat, then began to speak. It wasn't quite singing, but it wasn't quite speaking either. Franklin liked the way she spoke, and wanted to just go on listening to her. She was better than Preacher Sinclair, that was for sure. Her voice was welcoming and warm.

> *"Oh Goddess Mother*
> *May your gaze be kind*
> *And your heart open*
> *To those gathered here*
> *Bring them into your arms*
> *Let them know your blessings*
> *Comfort them*
> *And help them to see you and your works*
> *Every day*
> *We stand in the circle of your light*
> *We bring our open hearts to you*
> *We release our suffering from clenched fists*
> *We share the joy with one another that comes from living every day*
> *Welcome us, O Goddess Mother*
> *As we welcome each other*
> *Blessed be."*

Everyone in the circle responded with, "Blessed be."

Franklin didn't understand why he felt calmer. But everything settled down inside of him, like there had been something buzzing along his skin that had quieted.

Was Eddie gifted? Was she special, like him and Lexine?

"We're here to celebrate the life of our sister, Lexine, as well as to mourn her passing," Eddie continued. She led them in another prayer, where she called out a line, and they all repeated it. Franklin followed along as best he could, though he felt strange calling on goddesses and gods whose names he didn't recognize.

But he could tell that these people had their hearts in the right place. They all mourned Lexine. Franklin's chest felt weighted with grief. He was gonna miss her, how she'd teased him, as well as how she'd shared her spirits with him. She was the only one who'd really understood.

"Though our hearts are full of sorrow, we need to fill them with love," Eddie stated.

Here we go. Franklin didn't roll his eyes, but Eddie was starting to sound like Preacher Sinclair.

"We need to forgive," Eddie intoned. "Both ourselves for our failings, as well as those who have wronged us.

Forgive? Franklin nearly snorted. Not likely. He needed to kill that thing that had killed her, before it got to him and his cousin and the people he cared about. He didn't care about the sheriff and his ideas of Earl Jackson killing Lexine. It had been that spirit.

"Forgive," Eddie said again. "And let the blessings flow instead."

Franklin felt like Eddie was talking straight to him. How could he forgive? That thing wasn't even human. He didn't blame that Earl Jackson for Lexine's death, no, it was that creature. He knew it. It *hated* all those that were special, every person who brought light into the world and...

"Let go of hate," Eddie said. "Let go of the pettiness of hate. Let go of the pain and the fear."

Franklin paused. Hate was useful, right? His hate wasn't like the creature's. Not at all. He shifted from one foot to the other, uncomfortable. When he looked over at Eddie, he saw her swirling in light. It reminded him of Lexine's spirits: Franklin couldn't always tell what he was looking at, could just feel, sometimes, what they'd been. Like the soul of that old mill, or the spirits in the trees.

With Eddie, Franklin couldn't tell what she was, or was supposed to be. He just saw her in the light.

However, Eddie didn't see the lights around her. She moved one way, while they moved another. It was like they tried to push on her, but she didn't feel them.

Franklin realized that if Eddie had been following them, she'd have that same grace that Darryl had had.

If only she'd open her eyes and see.

Why couldn't she see? Maybe it was all the goddess worship. Franklin knew his gift came from God. Or maybe she'd just refused her gift, not wanting to deal with all her friends and relatives thinking she was crazy.

"Let's pray for healing," Eddie finally said.

Everyone dropped hands and folded their arms over their chests. Franklin did the same, feeling foolish. They chanted something low and smooth, syllables Franklin didn't understand.

While most people had their eyes closed, Franklin kept his open, curious.

Eddie walked around the circle, stopping in front of each person, then waving her hands in front of them. She didn't follow the same pattern. Sometimes she started at the head and followed the body down, sometimes she just did circles around their belly.

When Eddie got to Franklin, she focused on his heart.

The lights around Eddie grew brighter, and she moved in time with them for once, pushing warmth and strength inside of Franklin, healing something deep inside of him. He felt like he'd just taken a spoonful of warm honey, the sweetness lingering in his mouth while his insides were coated with golden light.

No wonder Lexine had kept coming back to this group if Eddie could sometimes tap into her powers and do that.

Maybe there was something to this pagan thing, but Franklin didn't think he'd be leaving the church anytime soon.

After the service, Franklin went over to talk with Eddie. "Thank you for having me, ma'am," he told her, shaking her hand. "And thank you for the healing."

"You're welcome to come back," Eddie said, beaming at him.

"Y'all know Lexine was special, right?" Franklin asked Eddie.

"She was," Eddie said. "She could always find the heart of the goddess, in whatever location we prayed in, whether it was here, or out in the fields, or in the woods near her place."

Franklin nodded. "She was good at seeing spirits. You could see 'em too, you know." Franklin wasn't sure exactly what Eddie's gift was, beyond the healing, but she could be doing everything better, that he knew.

"The goddess moves through me every day," Eddie said. "Showing me miracles and the divine."

It felt like an answer Eddie had rehearsed, like the same response Franklin gave folks when they asked if he was still single. "Well, that's nice," Franklin said. "But I think your goddess could show you more, if you was willing."

Eddie shook her head, smiling. "Lexine told me the same thing. But I'm too old to change my ways."

"I understand," Franklin said. And he did. Taking on a gift like his or Lexine's meant a lot of work. It also meant not fitting in, or not as well, with regular folk. But he'd always seen it as his duty, too—not something he could refuse. "Let me know if you change your mind," he added. He'd like to introduce Eddie to Adrianna. Eddie was like solid mountain, hefty, and not easily moved, while Adrianna floated through life. If they could work together, they'd probably be something even more special.

"Thank you," Franklin told Julie as they got in the car. "For bringing me there."

"You're welcome! I know the group really appreciated you coming, since you're Lexine's family and all."

They drove through the darkness in silence. The night had cooled off enough that they'd opened the windows, using the two-by-fifty-five AC.

"Do you think you'll want to come back?" Julie asked after a bit.

Franklin hesitated. "I'm not sure it's the right place for me," he said. He'd never tell her outright that he'd never go back.

"That's what I figured," Julie said. "It's Eddie, isn't it?"

"Whatdaya mean?" Franklin asked. He'd actually liked Eddie, even if she'd refused her gifts.

"Lexine said it was hard to see her closed off that way," Julie said.

Franklin shrugged. "A gift is sometimes a burden. It ain't always easy to carry."

"You see things for your gift, don't you?" Julie guessed. "Like Lexine."

"Maybe," Franklin said. "And maybe not." He wasn't admitting his gift to a pretty white nurse, especially since he did want to see her again.

Julie left it at that, and they didn't say much else until she'd dropped him off in the driveway.

"I wouldn't mind it," Julie called out her window.

"Wouldn't mind what?" Franklin asked.

"Wouldn't mind if you had a gift. Or if you called me again. Goodnight."

"Night," Franklin said, standing in his gravel driveway, watching her kick rocks as she climbed back up to the road.

Something cold moved down Franklin's back. Fearfully, he turned around.

Sweet Bess stood near the door, nosing along the base of the steps, not looking like she was going to attack him, but just hanging out in the yard.

Franklin watched her with relief.

His gift was back. And he bet, so was Mama.

CHAPTER 11

THE NEXT MORNING, FRANKLIN STOOD in his own tiny bathroom and removed the bandages from the wounds along his arms. The swelling had gone down a lot, and the skin looked only a little puckered under the stitches. It took some effort, and a long ruler from Mama's room, but he managed to pull off all the bandages on his back as well. Those wounds didn't look as swollen or bad. Maybe it was because it had just been glass, and not the creature.

Today, Franklin got to take a real bath. He didn't want to risk a shower, and wasn't sure how that spray would feel. But soaking in a tub? He could do that all morning long—that is, until he had to go to church.

After Franklin filled the tub, he gingerly set one foot in the water, then the other. *God*, the water felt so good. He crouched down and settled himself in. It was going to be another hot one today, but he still enjoyed the heat from the water, soaking into his skin, soothing his bones. His back itched a bit in the water, which he'd added Epsom Salts to. But it was a good itch, like muscles ready to be used after a rest.

With reluctance, Franklin got out of the tub when his alarm dinged. He patted himself carefully—nothing bleeding, nothing torn

—and got dressed in a good white shirt and gray trousers. He wasn't going to wear his suit today.

Sweet Bess was the first thing Franklin saw in the back when he opened his bedroom shade. *Goddamn it.* She was rooting around one of the stalks along the end of the row. She'd been the one who'd been knocking his corn down, one stalk at a time.

Franklin pounded on the window, but the sow didn't even look up. He debated opening it, sticking his head out and yelling at her, but he doubted that would do any good either.

Why was she destroying his crop? Was it because he'd slaughtered her that spring? Or was there some other reason?

"Morning, Mama," Franklin said as he came in the kitchen. Mama paced in front of the stove, agitated. She'd been fine the night before. What was going on? He still didn't know what she wanted from him, or why she'd been gone. Mostly, just impatient and angrier than usual.

Was it something to do with the creature? She sure was acting different.

Franklin knew Mama was worried about him, about what the thing was intending on doing to him. But she couldn't help and she didn't have any ideas how to stop it. He supposed that could agitate a body.

But somehow, it felt bigger. Like something more was occurring.

"Mama, I need to make breakfast," Franklin said when he approached the stove with his egg.

Mama kept pacing right in front of it: Two steps, turn, then two steps.

Franklin couldn't get near the stove without running into her, or maybe even *through* her, and he did *not* want to go through that again.

With a sigh, Franklin put away his eggs and just got out bread and peanut butter instead. It wouldn't be as satisfying without the egg, and without being fried, but it'd have to do. Since he'd been able to take a bath that morning (it had been so good—like proof that God still loved him) he didn't have a lot of time.

Mama didn't stop her pacing when Franklin stood next to the

stove, at the sink, washing off his plate. He kept a close eye on her, ready to move out of the way if she came too close.

Gloria was nowhere to be seen. Franklin figured he'd run into her later that day. He was gonna have to go back to Karl's place, see if he could take a look at Karl's fields, find out what the creature was so interested in.

For the first time in over a week, Franklin got out his bicycle. He checked the chain, making sure the gears still spun, before he climbed on and rode out the driveway.

Before Franklin had reached the end of the lane and gotten to the road, he was already panting. Maybe the really hot bath that morning hadn't been smart. He was tired and perspiring through both his undershirt and his shirt. It was like all the heat he'd absorbed that morning was now pouring back out his skin.

By the time Franklin reached the church, he wanted to turn around and just ride back home. His back ached from where his shirt stuck to his skin, his arms were on fire from supporting his weight on the handles, and he felt like an old man, out of breath and strength.

May peeled away from the group she'd been standing with and made a beeline toward Franklin. "What the hell do you think you're doing?" she demanded. She wore a sleeveless white blouse with a red skirt that would have been more appropriate for a Friday night than a Sunday morning.

"Going to church?" Franklin asked. What else was he supposed to be doing?

"We went by to pick you up," May said. "But you weren't there. Nothing was broken inside, but I had no idea where you'd gotten to."

"I'm okay," Franklin said, realizing that May had been scared that the creature had gotten him. "Really. It's okay."

"That's good, 'cause I'm about to take a wooden cooking spoon and beat your backside," May said, glaring.

"Could I get a ride home?" Franklin asked softly.

"We'll see," she said firmly. But she did take him by an uninjured part of his arm and tugged him along. "Let's get you inside, at least. You didn't pull any of your stitches, now, did you?"

"No, no, I'm fine," Franklin assured her. He gratefully stepped into the air conditioning of the church, letting the coolness bless his skin.

"So how was Miss Julie?" May asked with grin.

"Now wouldn't you like to know?" Franklin teased.

"I know nothing happened," May said. "You're too much of a school-boy, and the pair of you had just gone to a prayer meeting. So tell me about that."

Franklin wasn't sure what he could tell anyone about the meeting. "We met at this real nice lady's house, stood in a circle, held hands, and said prayers." That was the truth, at any rate.

"I thought she was taking you to a witch's coven or something," May said, disappointed. "I know it weren't no God-fearing group."

"Wait, you knew?" Franklin asked.

"Gottcha!" May said triumphantly. "I didn't know, not for sure," May admitted. "I knew Lexine had a group like that. I just bet it was the same one. So what was it like?"

Franklin shrugged. "Different. Nice. Those folks loved Lexine, and they were mourning her, in their own way."

"I miss her," May admitted.

"So do I," Franklin said. Lexine would never have shown up for church—once she'd come of an age when she didn't have to go, she'd stopped. But she'd show up afterward, over at Aunt Jasmine's house, to have dinner with them all, play with the kids, and hang out late into the night, talking.

"Has she found a better place?" May asked seriously.

"She ain't haunting me, if that's what you're asking," Franklin said.

"You remember that businessman? His company is now trying to get Ma to sell Lexine's land to them."

"Does Aunt Jasmine own that land, now?" Franklin asked as he followed May to a pew.

"She's going to," May said. "You remember Lexine had a will, right? You and Darryl missed the reading of it." May gave him a glare. "It was just a plain one, the kind you do over the internet. But it's legal, signed, and witnessed. Everything goes to Ma."

"That's good," Franklin said. Better that it all went to his aunt than the state.

"Ma don't want that place," May said. "None of us do, either. Do you want it?"

"Me? No," Franklin said. He remembered so long ago thinking about moving out there once. "No good fields for growing popcorn."

"You and your popcorn," May said with a sigh. "Any chance you gonna win the prize this year?"

"Yes," Franklin said. "My corn's coming in a bit earlier than Karl's," he said quietly. "More time to experiment, get it dried just right."

"What, you going for the tasting contest again? I figured you'd just enter the decorative one this year," May teased.

"I'm gonna win," Franklin told her firmly. "And the taste contest, not the 'make-a-pretty-display-of-corn' one." He was losing stalks, but so was Karl.

"You know we wish you all the luck," May said gently.

"I know. And I'll make you proud," Franklin declared.

And he would, too: not just of his corn-growing abilities, but how he got rid of the damn spirit as well, protecting his family.

THE SERMON WAS all about casting out the log in your own eye, instead of worrying about the speck of dust in God or your neighbor's eye. Franklin wasn't sure what it all meant. Eddie had been a lot more straightforward in her prayers, asking for healing and an open heart.

Even if it was to a goddess and not to God.

Franklin stood in line to shake the preacher's hand as he left the church.

"It was good to see you," the reverend said. He held onto Franklin's hand for another long moment. "You're looking better."

"I'm fine, reverend," Franklin said. "Really. It wasn't permanent."

"I'll come calling on you and your family later on this afternoon," the preacher announced. "Make sure your aunt's doing okay, after such a tragic loss."

"I'm sure she'll like that," Franklin said. He was planning on being gone early, getting May to drop him off near Karl's farm.

Maybe Franklin would be lucky and Karl would be gone, so he'd be able to just walk into Karl's field.

And maybe Sweet Bess would grow wings and fly above his field someday.

~

DESPITE HOW HOT the afternoon had turned, Franklin found he couldn't stay inside the house with everyone. It was too crowded, too noisy, too full of memories and grief. Aunt Jasmine had set up a table in the living room, underneath the big picture window facing the street, and filled the top of the table with pictures of Lexine and things that had been hers, both as a child and as an adult. It was like a shrine, or an altar, and it made Franklin nervous, like it was gonna attract the wrong kind of attention.

So Franklin sat out on the back steps, alone this time, watching May's boys throw a Frisbee back and forth.

Darryl came out to join Franklin after a bit. "How you holding up?" He'd taken off his good shirt and just wore his undershirt and good pants, his feet bare.

"Tired," Franklin admitted.

"I feel ya," Darryl said. He stretched his bandaged arms out. "I would've thought a few days off, around the house, would have been relaxing, but not with our kids."

"I keep wondering. How did that thing get into your truck?" Franklin asked, confused. "It just passed through when you tried to ram it."

"Haven't a clue. One minute I'm driving down the road, the next minute there's this whirling mass that's lashing out at me." Darryl shook his head. "I don't think I've ever moved so fast, getting out of my truck."

"Which road were you on?" Franklin asked.

"Sixty-two. Out past the Vanguards."

"Were you next to Karl's fields?" Franklin asked. It hadn't occurred to him before, but if Darryl was out on the highway...

"I may have been," Darryl said slowly. "You think there's a connection between him and the thing?"

Franklin nodded slowly.

"He's not controlling it, or something, is he? I'll kill him myself if he is," Darryl fumed.

"No, I think he's a victim, too," Franklin said quickly, trying to ward Darryl off.

"What, you telling me that redneck is special too?" Darryl asked, disbelieving.

"Naw, I don't think so. I think there's something in his field that's special, that the creature has been going after. Remember—it didn't attack Karl after he shot it—it came to find me," Franklin said.

"What the hell is in his fields?" Darryl asked.

"I don't know. But I intend to find out."

MAY REFUSED to drop Franklin off at Karl's place. "You need to go home and rest," she insisted. "You got black circles under your eyes, like you been up all night."

"I'm feeling better," Franklin assured May, though he had to admit he was still tired. "I promise to rest later this afternoon."

"You're going back to work tomorrow, ain't you?" May fumed.

"I don't have any more vacation," Franklin said. He really couldn't afford another day off. He was probably going to have to work six-day weeks for a while, and volunteer for overtime, to make up the money being out had cost him.

"Don't you end up working yourself into a grave, like your mama," May warned. "You got that pretty Julie now. Make sure you call her."

"Yes, ma'am," Franklin said, rolling his eyes. Mama had worked hard all her life. Franklin, too. He didn't know any other way.

As soon as May pulled out, Franklin got back on his bike and rode up to the four-lane highway and through town. He turned before he got to route sixty-two. Could he get through the back way to Karl's fields again? Using the route that Gloria had showed him the first time?

But there were kids playing in the yard of one of the houses, and Franklin didn't see another way. He hoped maybe Gloria would show up, show him the way, but she didn't.

So Franklin went back to the main road, then huffed his way out of town, back up route sixty-two, to Karl's place.

The tall gray house felt deserted. Karl's old Chevy still sat in the driveway, with the hood up. Loud cicadas cycled through their call in the fields. Franklin walked up the porch steps, his shoes echoing on the wood, then rang the doorbell.

No one answered.

Franklin knocked on the door, but still, no one came.

Maybe Karl was at the vegetable stand. Or maybe he was out back, working in his fields, and Franklin just couldn't see him from the house or the road. Or maybe the creature had him.

Franklin was pretty sure it wasn't the last one, or else Gloria would have been on Franklin's tail until he'd done something about it.

But where was Gloria? Franklin hadn't seen her since the night the creature had passed through him. Mama was back, and Franklin knew better than to start thinking maybe Gloria had just passed on and was no longer gonna bother him.

Franklin didn't want to go around the house, go into Karl's field uninvited. But maybe he could use the excuse of the creature to Sheriff Thompson, that Franklin was worried about Karl, worried for his safety.

As Franklin followed the well-laid brick walkway around the house into the back, Gloria appeared. She stared at Franklin, then walked away, through the thick, healthy tomatoes and squash plants, then disappeared into the rows of corn.

Franklin didn't want to trespass any more than he had been. But he knew he was going to have to follow her. He sighed, looking at all the bounty of Karl's fields, shaking his head. That man could grow anything. Then he squared his shoulders and followed Gloria into the field. He had his own duty to do.

Stalks of corn reached above Franklin's head. The air smelled dry and dusty. Green leaves curled gracefully from strong stems. Golden silks hung on the ends of the cobs. They were almost ready to harvest.

Franklin walked straight back. He knew how easy it was to get lost in a field: he couldn't see anything but the corn stalks around him and the blue sky above.

Gloria appeared again after Franklin walked through three more rows. He jumped, spooked.

She merely glared at him and pointed him off in a diagonal, closer to the road.

Franklin wished there was some way to better track where he was in the field, but these weren't his fields, wasn't his crop.

He was gonna get lost for sure.

Still, Franklin went off the direction Gloria pointed. She corrected him a couple more times.

Franklin was sweating again. The baked earth held in the heat, and no breeze stirred the leaves. It seemed like there was no end in sight, just tall stalks of corn, marching to the ends of the earth.

Suddenly, the rows opened up onto a flattened area. It looked like a mini-twister had hit the earth, swirling the corn in a big circle, then lifted away.

"What the hell?" Franklin asked, as he walked around it. It must have been the creature that had scattered the corn this way, that tell-tale cyclone.

Gloria appeared, her arms pulled tight against her ample chest. She didn't look angry for once. Instead, she looked worried. She looked down at her feet, then back up at Franklin and disappeared again.

Franklin walked over to where Gloria had been standing. A piece of twisted, thorny vine lay on the ground. It looked like a dried raspberry vine, covered in both large and small spikes.

Gingerly, Franklin picked it up. It twisted in his hand, startling him, making him cry out as he dropped it.

It lay still on the ground at his feet.

Was this where Karl had shot the creature? Blown off part of one of its whips? Is that what had caused this explosion?

Franklin squatted down and looked more closely at the ground. The stalks had been twisted out of the ground, shredded by the wind. But it looked like it had happened a long time ago, not just days ago. What had happened here? Was it an explosion?

Or had this been its nest?

"All right. Stand up slowly. And put your hands where I can see 'em,"

Karl. Shit.

Franklin raised his hands over his head before he turned around to face Karl. "What happened here?" Franklin asked calmly, though Karl held a twelve-gauge double-barrel shotgun aimed right at his face.

"Hell. I should have known it was you, sneaking around here," Karl said. He didn't move the gun an inch away, though, or relax his stance.

"Is this where you shot at something on Tuesday night?" Franklin asked. "Maybe filled it with rock salt?"

"I'm not telling you nothing," Karl declared. "Now move your ass. Back to the house. I'm calling the cops. Reporting you for trespassing."

"Karl, you know I ain't been stealing your crops. And I sure never made such a hole in your field," Franklin complained as he walked along the rows of corn.

Karl didn't reply, just prodded him with the barrel of his gun when Franklin slowed down to look over his shoulder.

Not even Gloria was there to help.

Inside the old house, Franklin found not only cobs of corn, but stalks, too, that had been rooted up and placed next to the dining room table. The wall of blue ribbons mocked him. Karl was gonna win this year too. Particularly if Franklin was stuck in jail.

His heart beat hard in his chest, but he wasn't about to run. That made no sense. But Karl wasn't really going to go through with turning him in, was he? He waited patiently while Karl called the cops.

"There's something about your fields, Karl," Franklin said when

Karl hung up, trying to stay calm. "Something that's attracting the creature."

"Just shut up," Karl said.

At least Karl put the gun down. But he stood in the wide archway between the front hall and the living room, his muscled arms across his skinny chest, his chin stuck out as belligerent as an ox.

"I ain't gonna try to run," Franklin told Karl.

"Like you could," Karl said disdainfully.

"But I needed to see what had happened. You know that Gloria led me to that place. I couldn't have found it on my own. What happened there?" Franklin asked.

Karl pressed his lips together stubbornly.

"You know that thing came and attacked me, after you shot it, right? It was a good thing you sent the sheriff out my way. I might've died, if he hadn't gotten me to the hospital."

"You and your creatures and your ghosts!" Karl exploded. "I hate 'em all! Everything was normal until you started competing against me."

"What do you mean?" Franklin asked, confused.

"I won that blue ribbon prize for years before you got interested in popping corn," Karl proclaimed, waving at his wall of ribbons. "I won it by working harder and smarter than all the other farmers around here, by tending my fields and making my land the best. Then you came along."

Franklin was sure that if they'd been outside, Karl would have spat onto the ground. As it was, his face looked all squinted up, like he'd kept something bad tasting on his tongue.

"Weird things started happening, right away, that first year. It was like my field was haunted or something. That part you saw blasted apart? It's always been a problem. Corn won't grow there, or it grows too fast and gets brittle."

"It's gotta be the creature," Franklin said. "What made it get so strong suddenly? Why'd it go after Lexine?" He paused, then asked, "Did that businessman, Earl Jackson, come to see you?"

Karl looked away at first, and Franklin was afraid he wouldn't answer. But eventually he turned his head back and said, "Yeah. Stupid businessman. Wanted to see about renting my fields. He told me he could grow anything in my fields. Swore up and down that he'd done some kind of analysis, and that the soil on my land was better than all the other farms. Not just this county, in all of Kentucky."

"Is it?" Franklin asked. He knew something was different about Karl's fields, that he always had the best yield.

Karl shrugged. "Could be." He sighed. "I know I worked hard enough at it. But...I don't think that was it. I think there was something else he wanted."

"The creature's nest," Franklin said.

"Would you just shut up about that creature?" Karl said. Then he paused. "He did ask about Lexine when he was here. Wanted to know if it was true that she could see spirits. Raise them."

"Really?" Franklin asked. He—and the cops and everyone else— had assumed that Earl Jackson had only cared about Lexine's land. "Lexine didn't raise spirits. She tried to calm them."

"Like I'd know," Karl said. "He took notes about things in his little notebook. It looked like it had a leather case around it."

"I doubt Sheriff Thompson will let me see it," Franklin said, musing to himself. "But I could ask if he's seen it, if there's a mention of Lexine and spirits."

Karl looked at Franklin. "You really do believe in these ghosts and spirits of yours, don't you." He sounded like he pitied Franklin.

"I do," Franklin said. How could he not believe what he saw? What he'd felt, those times he'd passed through a being? "And so should you. You got something in your fields, Karl, that's killing folks. And a ghost who might have loved you, who's trying to stop you from getting killed yourself."

Karl refused to say another word until the cops showed up.

CHAPTER 12

"I CAN'T BELIEVE HE WENT through with it," Franklin said, looking helplessly at his stained fingertips. Now the police had his prints.

If they ever printed that corn that had been next to Lexine's body, they'd know the prints was his.

"Don't fret about it," Darryl said. "Now you're just part of the family." He'd been the one Franklin had called to come and fetch him from the jail.

The sheriff hadn't been there. But Franklin had left a note for him, asking about the journal of Earl Jackson, and if it had mentioned Lexine or any spirits.

"My bike's still up at Karl's house," Franklin groused as they walked out of the county jail. "We're gonna have to stop by and get it."

"His place is on route sixty-two, right?" Darryl asked.

"Yeah," Franklin said slowly.

"Well, payback's a bitch," Darryl said as he got his shotgun out from under the seat and hung it in the gun rack in the back window.

"All Karl did was have me arrested for trespassing," Franklin said. "There's no need to go and shoot him." Maybe Franklin should have called May, but he'd been afraid all she'd have done for the entire drive home would be to yell at him.

"Wasn't him I was gonna hunt for," Darryl said. "Let's see what that creature of yours thinks about being blasted with rock salt."

"Karl already tried that," Franklin pointed out. "All he did was make the thing mad." He had the scars to prove it.

"Two steps ahead of you, Cuz," Darryl said with a grin. "It's rock salt, laced with antibiotics. If I get a good body shot, may actually kill it. Now, are you finished with your bellyaching so we can go get this thing?"

Franklin sighed and shook his head. He *knew* this was a bad idea.

He also knew, though, that if he insisted on Darryl driving him home, all Darryl would do is turn right around and go hunting it on his own.

"Only for a few hours, say, until sundown," Franklin said.

"We'll be home and three beers in by then," Darryl promised.

~

KARL WAS in his driveway this time when Darryl and Franklin drove up. He wiped his hands on his rag and picked up a socket wrench as they got out of Darryl's truck. "Didn't get enough of jail?" Karl sneered at Franklin. He stood loose and ready to fight.

"I left my bike here," Franklin said.

"I know. I threw it out on the highway," Karl said.

"You what?" Franklin said. He whirled to go check.

Darryl caught Franklin's arm. "He's lying, Cuz," Darryl said. "He's got it stored up here. He was waiting for you to come back and get it."

Franklin turned back to Karl. After another long moment, Karl gave him a huge grin, showing surprisingly white, straight teeth. "You sure are gullible."

"You had me arrested," Franklin pointed out.

"Sheriff said you'd refused to get printed before. I was just helping him out," Karl said, still grinning. "That way, I can prove it was you who stole my corn. Got your fingerprints on file."

"I ain't been stealing your corn, Karl," Franklin said.

"So you say. And what do you want?" Karl asked, addressing Darryl.

"You go hunting, right?" Darryl asked Karl. "Get your deer every year, don't you?"

"Sure," Karl said easily. "You do, too."

"I aim to go hunting in your fields for that creature," Darryl told Karl. "Can I have your permission to do that?"

Karl looked at Darryl, then at Franklin. "You got him convinced there's a thing out there too?"

Darryl rolled up one of his sleeves to show Karl his bandages. "I know it's there."

Karl looked from Franklin to Darryl and back again. "You two fools are so convinced I'm not about to stop you. Go waste your time."

"We have your permission?" Darryl asked again.

"Sure, sure," Karl said. "I think y'all are crazy, though."

Darryl walked back to his truck to get his shotgun. After he came back with it, Franklin turned back to Karl. "You want to come with?"

"I got too many danged things to do," Karl said heatedly. "But yeah. I do. Give me a sec."

Karl disappeared inside the house, then came out, rolling Franklin's bicycle, with a shotgun over his own shoulder. "Just in case you two idiots end up shooting at me."

Once they got to the field, Darryl crouched down and smoothed away the dirt at the edge of the corn field.

"What's he doing?" Karl asked.

"Tracking," Franklin said.

"Your whole family's weird," Karl declared.

Darryl entered the field, with Franklin and Karl on his heels. Unerringly, Darryl went directly to the nest that Franklin had found earlier. He circled the area, moving with that grace and speed Franklin had seen before.

Without warning, Darryl took off running.

"Where the hell's he going?" Karl asked as he raced after him.

"No idea," Franklin said.

Darryl moved effortlessly through the stalks of corn, flowing into spaces Franklin couldn't see, while Franklin got slapped in the face by leaves of corn.

It wasn't long before they lost him.

"Do you have any idea where he's going?" Franklin asked Karl. "Any other weird spots on your property?"

"The only weird thing on my property is you and your cousin," Karl said.

A shot rang out.

"This way," Karl said. "Back toward the house."

Franklin followed Karl as quickly as he could, trying to protect his arms and his face from the sharp-edged leaves. Hope filled him. Maybe they would be home and three beers in by sunset.

Darryl stood alone on the back lawn. He raised his shotgun triumphantly. "Got it!" he exclaimed.

Franklin looked around the property carefully. He didn't see anything there. "Got what?"

"I got it. Solid body hit. I'm sure of it," Darryl said.

"You're lying," Karl said. "You just fired a shot up in the air."

"I don't lie. Not about hunting," Darryl said coldly.

"Where is it, then?" Franklin asked. He went over to the spot Darryl pointed to.

Another of those long, brown vines lay twisting on the ground. "You winged it," Franklin said, dread filling his gut. "I just hope there was enough antibiotics to make it go off and lick its wounds, not attack someone else."

"Hell yeah," Darryl said. "I mighta killed it."

Franklin's cell phone buzzed in his pocket. He fished it out and looked at the caller ID.

Ray.

"You didn't," Franklin said.

~

ALL THREE OF them piled into the front of Darryl's truck, Franklin in the center again. Grim and silent, Darryl sped his way to the Sorrels' place. Fortunately, the gate was open.

The creature was still there. Its long whips flayed the paths Adrianna had made Ray build, sending a hailstorm of sharp stones everywhere. Fallen branches, twigs, and bark lay twisted on the ground: Adrianna's tree men no longer stood. All the artwork was shattered, from the pressed glass pieces to the mermaid to the pinwheels.

"Shoot it!" Franklin told Darryl.

Darryl fired off a shot as it was disappearing. The shot passed clean through and imbedded itself in the fence behind it.

Franklin raced over to where Adrianna lay on the ground, half supported by Ray. "Call an ambulance!" he shouted.

Adrianna's face was all torn up. One of her arms didn't seem to be attached right either. "Help's on the way," he told her and Ray. "Hang on."

"But it'll be beautiful on the other side," Adrianna said weakly.

"Don't go," Ray whispered. "Please, my lady of light. Don't leave me."

"I can't stay," Adrianna whispered. She turned her gaze away from Ray to Franklin. "You must fight it with love. Anything else will kill you too."

"No, Miss Adrianna," Franklin said. "You can't die. You can't let it win."

"It won't win. Not while there's still love in the world," Adrianna whispered.

"She was driving it back," Ray said. "You were so strong." He looked up at Franklin. "Then it attacked me."

"I couldn't help it," Adrianna said. "I couldn't let it get to you. I lost the love."

"I can't lose you," Ray said.

"You won't. I'll still be here, waiting for you," Adrianna said. "And..." she paused, blinking, then gave a great exhale.

And she was gone.

∾

When Sheriff Thompson arrived, he made a beeline for Franklin and pulled him aside. "What the hell happened?"

The pain of Adrianna's passing felt like a solid weight, pressing on Franklin's lungs, making it hard to breathe. "We went hunting the thing. Darryl winged it, in Karl Metzger's fields. So it came here."

"It came here?" the sheriff asked. "Why?" He still sounded like he didn't believe anything Franklin was saying.

Franklin nodded. "The last time Adrianna tried to fight it, using her power lines, she failed. It ended up being able to suck up a lot of the power she'd raised, and grew stronger. Maybe it decided to try that again, see whether she'd make it stronger, heal it."

"I'm sorry for your loss," Sheriff Thompson said. "She was good people."

"She was," Franklin said. "The best."

"You left me a message, asking about Earl Jackson's notebook?" the sheriff asked.

Franklin tried to put away his grief. "Yes, sir. According to Karl, Earl Jackson wasn't just seeing Lexine about her land. He also was asking about her abilities, whether she could raise spirits."

"Is it possible this Earl Jackson brought this thing with him?"

"That's what I've been wondering. Was it part of him? And how did it get separated, and start attacking people?" Franklin shook his head.

"Now, I know your cousin was a witch," the sheriff said. "Praying to other gods and like that."

Franklin held onto his temper. It wouldn't do him no good if he decked the sheriff. But he was gonna have to walk away if the sheriff kept talking like that.

"I've been going through Earl Jackson's notebook. There's incantations to a goddess Bridget? Spells for demons. Prayers," the sheriff said.

"I wouldn't know anything about those," Franklin said. "But I know someone who would."

It wasn't the best excuse to call Julie, but at least it was something.

FRANKLIN SHOWED up for work the next morning at the Kroger. His uniform scratched over the still healing cuts on his back, and he still didn't feel like he was up to full strength. But he couldn't stay away much longer, not if he still wanted to have a job.

Charlene pulled Franklin to the side just after his morning break. They went up to her command center, where the black and white video screens showed the different parts of the store. Charlene wore her usual uniform—white shirt, black pants, and a big black belt with lots of pouches on it. She sat heavily in her chair, crossed her arms over her chest, and stared at Franklin, still standing in the doorway.

"You been on the police scanner," she told him. "Too much for my liking."

Franklin shrugged. "It weren't all my fault," he pointed out.

"You even got arrested," she said coldly.

"I still can't believe Karl Metzger went through with that," Franklin complained. "I was trespassing, yes. But it was for a good cause."

"You're getting on the wrong side of the law," Charlene said. "And as your friend, I have to tell you, that worries me."

"Charlene, I'm not a criminal," Franklin protested. Where was this coming from? Why was she giving him such a hard time?

"There's been talk of putting you on probation," she told him sternly.

"What?" Franklin asked, steamed. "Why would you do that?" Probation meant something would go in his employee record, and his file with Kroger was empty. He'd never been cited for being late or not combing his hair or breaking any of the rules.

"I don't like what's been happening," Charlene warned. "So you make sure it stops happening."

"Yes, ma'am," Franklin said bitterly. He'd thought he and Charlene were friends. Obviously, he'd been wrong. "Anything else?"

"Franklin, I'm doing this for your own good," Charlene said. "You'll thank me for it, if you get yourself turned around."

"Yes, ma'am. I gotta go back to work," Franklin said, backing up out of the office and going back down to the floor, where he tackled cleaning out the dried nuts stand.

Why was Charlene being like that? Was it really because of him being arrested? Or was it something else?

Franklin chewed on the problem all day. Should he go talk to Charlene? Ask her what was going on? Or had he been as naïve as his cousins always claimed, and had she never been his friend?

In the end, he decided not to say anything. It would be too embarrassing for both of them.

Still, at the end of the day, as Franklin was getting ready to leave, he found Julie waiting for him at the end of checkout lane number three.

"I didn't know you was here," Franklin told Julie as he came up.

"Really?" Julie asked. "I told the store manager that I was here to pick you up."

"Huh. Well, I'll only be a minute to change," Franklin said. When he turned, he saw Charlene standing over near the produce section, staring at him.

No, staring at *Julie*.

He didn't know how Charlene had found out about Julie. But Charlene knew everything about everyone. He should have realized.

And he should have known that Charlene was sweet on him. Thinking back, it was obvious.

He was the only one who'd ever been allowed up in her command center.

He'd have to patch up that bridge later.

Right now, he had to get changed and walk up the street to the sheriff's office.

~

"YOU THINK that businessman was calling demons?" Julie asked as they walked slowly up the hill to the Judicial Center, past the real estate agency that was in another of the turn-of-the-century store fronts on Main Street. Twilight approached, and the light had dimmed, but the air still held the heat of the day.

"Might have been," Franklin said. "You know it was a creature that hurt me, right?" His heart was pounding in his chest. He blamed it on the hill they was climbing, ignoring how his hands might be shaking a little, too.

Julie nodded. "I'd heard. Attacked your cousin, and killed a couple people now, right?"

"Yeah. I gotta stop it. Somehow," Franklin blurted out.

"Why you?" Julie asked.

It wasn't part of his duty, like helping ghosts pass. But it was, still, at the same time. Franklin took a deep breath and gulped some air before he finally replied, "Because I can see it."

"And most folks can't?" Julie asked.

Franklin shook his head. "Not unless I help 'em."

"I think it's very brave of you," Julie said.

"And a little crazy?" Franklin asked, trying to tease, to get them out of the serious mood they were in.

"Maybe a little crazy," Julie admitted. She looked over him and smiled. "But I happen to like a little crazy."

Before Franklin could reply they were at the walkway to the tall brick judicial center. The air seemed to chill as they approached. Franklin knew it was just the AC leaking from the building, but it still made him shiver slightly once.

"You ever been arrested?" Julie asked.

Franklin sighed as he held open the glass doors for her. "Once. Yesterday. By Karl Metzger, for trespassing in his fields."

"Really?" Julie said. "Just yesterday?"

"I'm not a criminal," Franklin said crossly.

"Hey, it's okay. I was just curious," Julie said. "I've never been arrested either, but I'm a cute white girl and can talk my way out of most things."

A long white counter bore a gold plaque that said *Reception*. An older, larger white woman in a blue uniform stood behind it. She barely glanced up from her report when they approached. Behind her stood a wide open office, full of desks that were empty.

"Julie Horton," Julie announced. "I'm here to see the sheriff."

"We have an appointment," Franklin added.

The woman opened up a visitor's log, swung it around and slid it across the counter to them. "Sign in, please."

When Franklin pushed the book back to the officer, she looked up again. "Wait here."

Julie looked around. "It looks like a regular office," she said quietly.

"What were you expecting? Something with a jail cell in the front?" Franklin teased.

"Maybe," Julie said. "I don't know. More gritty? Or maybe even more clean? Something."

"Not just an ordinary place, where ordinary people go to work?"

Julie grimaced. "I know, I know. People say that about the ER all the time, too. They think it should look like the ones they've seen on TV. Not a place where just us regular folk work."

"I would think a hospital would be exciting, at least," Franklin said. "You're saving people's lives. All I have to worry about is spilled fruit or cleaning up the aisles."

"It can be exciting," Julie admitted. "But those times are rare. It's more than just a job, but—"

"You still wouldn't do it if you won the lottery," Franklin filled in.

"Exactly!" Julie turned to smile at Franklin just as Sheriff Thompson came in the room.

He cleared his throat. "This way," he said, opening the door at the end of the counter for them.

"Thank you," Julie said.

Franklin just nodded at the sheriff as he led them back to his office.

"Put these on," the sheriff instructed, holding out a box of black gloves.

Julie slid on her gloves with a professional snap. Franklin fumbled his on, the forefingers twisted, cutting off the circulation. He could already feel his palms sweating.

Franklin sat gingerly on the edge of the visitor's chair, but he gave Julie a reassuring smile.

The sheriff took a small, black notebook out of a large plastic bag —an evidence bag, Franklin realized with a start. That was kind of cool.

"Don't tear or attempt to destroy this, or I'll have your heads,"

Sheriff Thompson warned Julie as he handed her the notebook. "Both of you."

Franklin didn't think it had been possible for Julie to sit more at attention, but she did. "It's okay," he said, reaching over to lay his hand briefly on her arm. "Just look at what's written in there."

Julie flipped open the notebook. Franklin looked over her shoulder. The first page seemed very much like a prayer Eddie would recite, asking the goddess Bridget for patience and kindness, to open his mind and refresh his spirit.

But the next one wasn't about a goddess. It was addressed to a demon, asking for his whirling strength to defeat his enemies and cast them before him.

Franklin glanced up at Julie at the same time she looked at him. She pressed her lips together and shook her head, then returned back to the book, flipping through the pages.

The pattern repeated, prayers to the softer gods and goddesses, followed by incantations to bring forth devils and demons.

Toward the end, Julie stopped and put her fingers toward her mouth. "Oh my," she said. "This one. This spell. This isn't right."

"What do you mean?" Sheriff Thompson asked. "It isn't written right?"

"No, not really. It's—it's twisted. All the others were separate. This is the first one that's combined, both the goddess and the devil." Julie shivered. "This—this is blasphemy."

Franklin was surprised to hear Julie use that term. Wasn't that only for God?

"He wasn't a good man," Julie said, shaking her head. "He was trying to invoke the basest spirits to do his bidding. And he...he offered a life, here. A sacrifice. To bring forth his demon."

"Do you think he succeeded?" Franklin asked. "Is that where our creature came from?" Was he really the one to kill Lexine? Did her death bring that creature into being?

Julie shrugged. "I don't know. I never really thought any of this was possible. What he wanted, what he was trying to bring forth. I mean, prayer can change the world, but I'd never thought it'd do this."

Franklin nodded. "Maybe it wasn't the spell, by itself, that created the spirit. Maybe it was the combination of Lexine's ability to see spirits, along with her death."

"Could Lexine call spirits to her?" Sheriff Thompson asked.

"I don't think so," Franklin said, addressing the sheriff in surprise. He couldn't call ghosts to him. "She always said they just found her."

"So maybe Earl Jackson did the calling," Julie said. "And the creature found them, because of Lexine."

"Lexine would never have allowed Earl to call something like that on her property," Franklin said. But maybe the businessman hadn't done it in her living room, but while he was in his truck, parked out at the end of her driveway.

"Earl's body showed some signs of a struggle," the sheriff commented. "He'd been scratched on his face, under those gouges. And Lexine had his skin under her fingernails."

"So they fought first and then the thing attacked?" Franklin guessed. Had Earl Jackson sacrificed Lexine to fully bring forth the creature?

"I don't think we'll ever know," Sheriff Thompson said. "Not unless you have some kind of time machine or magic seeing ability."

Franklin shook his head. "No such luck, I'm afraid. And how the creature came into being don't really matter now. The question is, how do we get rid of it?"

"I don't know," Julie said. "I've never known anyone who performed this kind of magic, before." She looked frightened.

"It's okay," Franklin reassured her, patting her arm again. "Would any of the others in your group know?"

"We can ask Eddie," Julie said.

"Let's get going, then," the sheriff said. He stood up.

"Now?" Franklin asked. He hadn't had dinner yet, and he was so tired from his first day being back at work.

"Now." The sheriff paused. "I just want you to know that I don't necessarily believe in what y'all are saying, that this is some kind of magical creature, called by this businessman after he'd killed your cousin. However." The sheriff stroked his mustache with his thumb and forefinger. "However. Something killed Adrianna. And that tramp out in the woods. The same thing damn nearly killed you, and it beat up your other cousin pretty bad. It isn't killing anyone else. We don't normally have more than two, three killings a year. I need to get ahead of this thing."

"Then let's go see Eddie," Julie said, also standing, stripping off her gloves. "We'll pick some food up on the way," she promised Franklin.

Franklin sighed. But he knew the sheriff was right. This thing had to be stopped.

But Eddie had refused her power. He suspected she'd refuse to help with this as well.

CHAPTER 13

EDDIE PALED AS SHE READ through the incantation. She stood in front of the mantel of her fireplace in her living room, while the sheriff, Julie, and Franklin all sat on the white and green patterned chairs and matching sofa. She looked like something out of a movie, with her wild white curls standing on end, wearing all blue and green underwater colors, from her shirt to her skirt to the big scarf she had wrapped across her shoulders.

"You're saying this man may have *called* this thing? Truly brought it into being?" Eddie asked.

"Maybe," the sheriff said. He looked uncomfortable. "I still don't rightly believe what y'all have been saying," he said, shooting a dark look at Franklin. "But I don't think it's just a wild animal killing people. It's got too much purpose. It's got to be directed, or self-directing."

"Why y'all here?" Eddie asked. "What do you expect me to do about it?"

"Do you know how to kill it, ma'am?" Julie asked.

"No, I don't," Eddie said immediately.

Franklin knew she was lying. "There's got to be something we can do, in that place of yours, out back."

Eddie turned to glare at Franklin. "Even if there was, absolutely not. You may not use my sacred space for this type of work."

"But ma'am, we need to stop this creature," Franklin replied.

"Mine is a place of peace," Eddie said sharply. "What this man brought forth is the opposite. It only hates. It consumes. It has no companions, only enemies and competitors. It's the perfect *familiar* for a success-obsessed businessman," she added with disgust.

"Then how do we get rid of it?" Julie asked.

"I wish I knew," Eddie said, softening. "I truly don't know what y'all are gonna do. But it feeds on hate. You need to approach it with love."

Franklin exchanged a glance with Julie. He'd told her that was what Adrianna had said, before she'd died. "But what type of love is strong enough?" Franklin asked. "I mean, love just isn't as strong as a gun or a knife, right?" Adrianna and her lines of power ripped from the very earth hadn't been enough. The creature had still survived.

"It isn't the weapon that's been formed out of love," Eddie said. "It's the love itself. It's gotta be great enough." She sighed. "And I don't love enough." She looked at Franklin. "I don't believe enough."

Franklin nodded. He glanced over at Sheriff Thompson, who had his lips twisted and pressed together hard. Franklin could practically hear the words the sheriff was saying in his head, *Well, this was a waste of time.*

"Julie, dear, can you come with me, for a moment?" Eddie asked. Julie nodded and rose.

"Kill it with love. Bah," Sheriff Thompson said as soon as the two women were out of earshot. "I can't believe she said that."

"It's what Adrianna said. And Billy, too," Franklin said.

The sheriff paused, stroking his great brown mustache, his beady eyes staring a hole in the carpet. "You think this thing lives in Karl Metzger's fields."

"Yes, sir," Franklin replied, not sure where the sheriff was going.

"And you're positive it's what hurt you, killed Adrianna," the sheriff continued.

"I'd swear on my Mama's grave," Franklin replied.

"What did your cousin use the last time, to damage it?"

"Rock salt, mixed with antibiotics." Was the sheriff finally starting to believe?

Sheriff Thompson stood up. "That's it, then. I'm tired of waiting for it to attack again. I'm just going to get a bunch of deputies together and go find it," the sheriff declared. "Serve a warrant to Karl Metzger, march across his field, and shoot every five paces. We're bound to shoot it."

"You're likely to get yourselves or someone else killed," Franklin said, appalled.

The sheriff glared at him. "It's my duty to protect the citizens of this county."

Franklin shook his head. More than likely, the sheriff had just signed Franklin or Darryl's death warrant, particularly if he and his men only winged the thing and it came looking for revenge again.

ON THE DRIVE back into town, Julie was quiet, thoughtful. "Can I ask you something?" she finally asked as they crossed the county line, back into Wesley County. The night stretched out around them, hiding the endless fields that ran next to the road. Big semis blew by the little car, rocking it from side to side. They kept the car windows open to keep them cool.

"Sure," Franklin said. He'd been bracing himself for this. Whatever Eddie had said to Julie had left her shaken.

"Is this thing really that dangerous?" she asked.

"You know it's killed at least two people, right?" Franklin replied. Julie had to know that.

"I know, it's just…it doesn't seem real."

"You saw the gouges on my arms," Franklin said. He wasn't sure what Julie was really asking about. She *knew* this thing was deadly.

"Eddie said, she said she wanted me to protect myself," Julie confessed. "She gave me her altar knife."

"That three-sided thing?" Franklin asked. "Damn." He shivered. That knife had bothered him. It hadn't killed people, but it was deadly. He just knew it. What had Lexine thought about it? Had it bothered her too?

"I didn't want to, but she was so insistent that I take it," Julie explained.

"The creature won't come after you," Franklin said. "It only comes after those folks who are special." That made him happy that Julie would be safe no matter what.

"So it went after Lexine, and it'll come after you," Julie pointed out. "What happens if I'm nearby?"

"It only attacked Adrianna, not Ray," Franklin said. God, he still couldn't believe she was dead.

"Eddie don't really believe in this thing, you know," Julie said. "She's afraid that it's a product of y'all; that your negative thoughts are why it's manifesting."

"I know. She doesn't really believe in anything." She'd refused her gift. Which would probably keep her safe from the creature.

Franklin didn't think the exchange was worth it.

"So what do you love?" Julie asked.

Franklin sighed. He'd been thinking about that for a while. He'd loved his Mama, but then she'd died. He loved his family, when they weren't driving him crazy.

And he loved growing popping corn—tall stalks of corn, leaves rustling in the breeze, fine silks on the top of each cob jutting proudly from the stem. How the pale kernels grew golden in the sun and the rain. He loved the science of drying the cobs, too, slowly baking them to remove the moisture.

Then the popping. The anticipation of the kernels, sizzling in lard, waiting until it was just right. How would the wings grow on each of the kernels? Would there be button kernels instead? How thick was the hull? Had he gotten it right?

"Lots of things," Franklin finally told her. "How about you?"

"I know you're lying," Julie replied. "But that's okay. We only just met. I don't expect you to tell me. But as long as you know, yourself, I think you'll be fine."

Franklin could only hope she was right.

~

"Take it," Julie insisted, handing the knife, hilt first, to Franklin.

"I really don't want that thing," Franklin said, pressing back against the door of the car.

"Please," Julie said, her eyes bright even in the dark. "It'll make me feel better."

With a sigh, Franklin reached out and took the knife. Despite the heat of the night, it still felt cold and heavy in his hands. "I'll take it, but I ain't gonna use it," he told her.

"I hope you won't need to," Julie said sincerely. She reached out and briefly touched his cheek. "Take care. Be safe."

Franklin pressed into her fingers. "I will. You too."

He stood in the center of his driveway as she peeled out. The quiet of the night came back, spiked with the music of the cicadas and crickets. A few stars shone down, breaking through the lights of the town. Yet Franklin felt restless, driven to do...something. He wasn't sure what, or why.

Inside the house, both Mama and Gloria were waiting for Franklin in the kitchen.

With a loud *thump*, Franklin dumped the knife on the kitchen table. Suddenly, his night felt freer again.

Worry spilled out from both ghosts, stifling and thick, setting Franklin's back up. "What are you worried about?" Franklin asked as he took a seat at the table. "About me? Or that thing?"

Mama and Gloria both glared at the knife. They'd both also pressed themselves back from the table, as if they was scared.

"So it's the knife," Franklin said, picking it up and looking at the long blade. It sucked up all the light in the kitchen, including the ghostly glow of his visitors. Power flowed from the metal into his fingers and up his arm. The night grew still while Franklin grew stronger.

"This knife, here, it can hurt you, can't it," Franklin said. He felt eerily calm, like the blade had shaved away all his usual nervousness.

Mama slowly nodded.

"And the creature? Can this knife hurt it?" Franklin asked. Maybe taking it from Julie had been a good idea. It sure made him feel good.

Neither Mama or Gloria replied.

They didn't know.

Maybe that was why the knife hadn't bothered Lexine. It was just for ghosts.

"You know I could use this thing," Franklin said casually. "Put one or both of you out of your misery. Get you to pass on, stop haunting me."

Mama heaved her chest impressively, as if giving Franklin an exasperated sigh. A single word floated from her.

Cheater.

"Using the knife is cheating? Pushing you beyond? Instead of solving your issues? Doing my *duty?*" Franklin asked, his temper rising. Damn it, he was tired of all the hauntings and the creature and everything. He just wanted some kind of normal life again, where Lexine wasn't dead, and neither was Adrianna.

Mama just glared at Franklin, while Gloria looked thoughtful.

With an effort, Franklin released the knife, dropping it back onto the table, letting loose the power in his hand. "I won't use the knife, Mama. Not on you. I promise."

Gloria couldn't actually make him a thief when it came to the most important thing in his life, growing popping corn.

This knife, this thing of power, wouldn't turn him into a cheater, either.

FRANKLIN CALLED Darryl from the Kroger the next day, during his first break. He'd stepped outside the store, into the back alley, where he'd at least have a little privacy. Large bales of cardboard boxes that had been flattened lay neatly stacked next to the dumpsters. The sun beat down on the tiny alley. Franklin hung next to the brick wall, trying to stay in the shade.

"The sheriff's being an idiot," Franklin told Darryl. "He's gonna get one of us killed."

"Whatcha mean?" Darryl asked.

Franklin told Darryl the plan the sheriff had about gathering deputies and going hunting this thing. "He'll end up just winging it, right? So it'll come directly after us."

"Then we gotta be prepared," Darryl said. "You know it'll go to your place first."

"Maybe," Franklin said. He hadn't thought about that. "How are we gonna fight it?" He still didn't think they could just use love.

"I'm thinking maybe the problem has been the shotguns," Darryl said.

"What?" Franklin shook his head. Of course, Darryl would be thinking about weapons.

"It's a whirling thing, right?"

Franklin nodded, shivering in the heat. He could still see it in his mind's eye, like a dust devil, with poisonous whips.

"So maybe it needs something that'll penetrate it more slowly. Like an arrow."

"I don't understand," Franklin complained. "And I don't know how to use a bow."

"It's okay. I do."

"Now *you're* the one gonna get us killed," Franklin said. "No. We gotta come up with a better plan on how to defend ourselves."

"Well, when you come up with one, I'll be all ears," Darryl said. "In the meanwhile, I'm getting more ammo ready," he added, hanging up.

Franklin sighed. Darryl was probably right—that thing would come after him first. And while Darryl's plan was terrible, at least he had one.

Franklin needed to come up with some kind of plan soon.

THE FUNERAL for Adrianna was at the Unitarian church across town, one that Franklin had never been to before. It didn't have crosses or pictures of saints, just scenes of regular folks, helping each other. The floor was made from a fancy marble that clicked or clacked with every step. Wide wooden beams held up the roof, making the sanctuary feel even more open. Families huddled closer together on the pews, friends sitting right beside their neighbors, 'cause the place felt so big.

Franklin sat with Charlene and the others from the store, though Charlene made sure that a couple of folks sat between her and Franklin. None of his cousins had come: They hadn't known the Sorrels as well. But at least half the town was there.

The sermon was nice enough, though Franklin didn't know any of the hymns they sang. But lots of people stood up and talked about Adrianna, telling stories about her life, her acts of kindness, how they'd all miss her and her crazy schemes.

After the service, they all went downstairs to the community room. That, at least, felt the same as the one at Franklin's church, with similar round tables, cookies, coffee, and tea.

Franklin went to say hello to Ray. "I'm so sorry," Franklin said, shaking Ray's hand.

"I know," Ray said. "You make sure you take care of this thing. You stop it from killing anyone else."

"I will," Franklin promised. He had no idea how, but he would.

KARL CAME up to Franklin as he was getting ready to leave the church. Franklin almost didn't recognize him, wearing a gray-green suit that hung on him, like it had been made for a larger man, his hair washed and hanging down around his shoulders, with a cream-colored shirt and black tie.

It figured. Karl even dressed better than he did.

"Hey, jailbird," Karl said, reaching out his hand to shake Franklin's first.

"You ain't never gonna let that go, are you?" Franklin asked, surprised, but still taking Karl's hand. "I didn't know you knew Adrianna." Karl had been at the Sorrels' parties, like most of the folks in town, but Franklin hadn't known they'd been friends.

Karl shrugged. "Everyone knew Adrianna."

Franklin nodded. She'd always been talking with everyone at the store, asking people how they were and how their day was going, even if she didn't know them. "You know the sheriff's planning on coming after the creature," Franklin told Karl softly. "At your farm." Even if Karl was his rival, he still deserved to know.

"You're shitting me," Karl replied. "Dang it! How the he-heck does he intend on doing that? He can't even see it. I don't even think it's real."

"He says he's gonna get a warrant, do a line shoot." Franklin shook his head. At least the sheriff had enough discipline over his men that they wouldn't go shooting each other.

"That even legal?" Karl asked.

"Sheriff thinks so," Franklin said. "'Course that means the thing'll just come after Darryl or me."

"Really?" Karl said. "You sure?"

"Every time it's been injured, it comes looking for revenge," Franklin told Karl.

"I wouldn't want to be in your shoes," Karl said, shaking his head.

"Why, thank you," Franklin said dryly. They stood in silence for a moment, watching a group of young women walk by. "Why does that thing like your fields so much, Karl?" Franklin asked. "Do you even know?"

"I didn't remember until just recent," Karl admitted. "When Adrianna and Roy first came to town, they tried to buy my fields. Adrianna said they was the most powerful in town. The place they got was the second most powerful."

"You think that thing is feeding off your land somehow?" Franklin asked. No wonder the thing kept going back to Karl's fields, why it had attacked Adrianna. It was drawn to that power.

"Yeah. That businessman, too, wanted my fields." Karl paused, then added, "My popping corn's better than yours."

"No, it ain't," Franklin replied automatically, stung by Karl's statement.

"It is," Karl insisted. "And it's because there's something special in my land. I've seen how you treat your fields, how much precision you use in drying your corn. You should be winning the prize. But you never will."

"Bull," Franklin said heatedly. He looked over his shoulder, then looked down again, embarrassed at the older black woman giving him a dark look for swearing. "I will win it. This year, too."

"If you win, it'll only be because someone's been stealing so much of my crop," Karl said seriously. "It ain't that you ain't good, Franklin. You are. You're the best competitor I ever had. But I know, I *know*, there's something special in my land, especially since this summer."

Franklin nodded, swallowing down the bitterness rising in his throat. He wasn't ever gonna beat Karl, was he? Everything was stacked against him, as always.

"Don't take it so hard," Karl said, patting Franklin's back. "All that I got that's special is that field. While everyone in town knows you're special, all on your own."

Franklin paused, turning to look at Karl. He'd never thought of it that way before.

Karl continued. "Most folks never gave me much credit for what my farm produced. They knew it was the land. Could throw seeds across the stones there and they'd grow." Karl sighed. "I work damn hard. You believe it. But nobody else does. None of my great crops come from *me*. No one ever thinks I'm talented or special. It's just the land. Not me."

"They're still great crops," Franklin pointed out.

"Yeah, and I wouldn't trade that. But I just...I wish I could take a bit more credit, you know? You earn that second-place ribbon. I don't know if I earn mine or not."

Franklin thought about that for a long time after Karl left the room. He'd always thought he wanted to exchange his life for Karl's.

For the first time, Franklin wasn't so sure.

JUST OUTSIDE THE CHURCH, Franklin saw Charlene talking to some of the checkers from the Kroger. He walked over toward them, pleased to see Charlene not only didn't turn her back, but instead, excused herself from the group and walked toward him as well.

"Morning, Miss Charlene," Franklin said. "You look nice." And she did, in her white blouse with the frills down the front and a tight black skirt. She still only wore work makeup, enough to be pretty but not stand out. Large gold hoops, like what Mama wore, dangled from her ears.

"Morning, Franklin. You still look like shit," Charlene said with a smile. "You ever sleep?"

Franklin shook his head. "Not much. I'm hoping that things get settled soon though." Either he was gonna take care of the creature, or it would get him.

"I'm glad you came to the funeral," Charlene said.

"Why wouldn't I?" Franklin asked.

"You was there when she was killed," Charlene said. "I figured you might be too guilty."

"What, are you thinking I killed her or something?" Franklin asked. He kept hold of his temper, though, hoping Charlene wasn't accusing him of anything else.

"No, I don't," Charlene said seriously. "I know you did everything you could to help that poor woman."

Franklin nodded. He just wished there was something he could have done, even if he'd gotten over there earlier.

"You know, the sheriff don't really believe in all your talk of a creature," Charlene said.

"I know," Franklin said with a sigh. How could the poor man? He'd never seen it. Hell, most of the time no one believed Franklin's ghosts, including Charlene, and ghosts was harmless. Thinking that something that most folks couldn't see was deadly was just asking too much. "But he's still going after it," Franklin added.

"Really?" Charlene asked. She had that gleam in her eye, wanting to know more. "Details."

Franklin happily obliged, telling her about the sheriff's plan to shoot up Karl's fields.

"So that's why he canceled his deputy's leave. Wanted him to come in, instead," Charlene said, nodding.

"Really? He canceled leave? That's just wrong," Franklin said.

"Don't I just know it. Say, have you heard—" Charlene broke off as Sheriff Thompson's Crown Vic pulled into the parking lot, the lights on top flashing. "What's he doing here?"

"Beats me," Franklin said, though sweat broke out all across his shoulders. Had someone else been attacked? Was there someone else dead?

The sheriff got out of his car, leaving the lights flashing. He walked directly toward Franklin. "You thought you were so clever, not giving us your prints, that first time," the sheriff complained as he bore down on Franklin.

"What do you mean?" Franklin asked, backing up.

"I'm here to arrest you for the murder of your cousin, Lexine. Now, turn around, hands behind your back," the sheriff directed.

Franklin turned, helpless. What the hell? Why was he suddenly a murder suspect?

Then he remembered the cob of corn, with his fingerprints on it.

They must have finally gotten around to matching his prints to it.

When Franklin turned back around, the cold metal of the handcuffs cutting into his wrists, the first thing he saw was Charlene, backing away and shaking her head.

He'd lost her friendship, for sure. Hopefully, he still had a job.

"Did you really have to do that?" Franklin complained as the sheriff removed the handcuffs once Franklin was seated in the back of the sheriff's car. The seat felt sticky under Franklin's good suit, and the car stank of sweat, stale French fries, and spilled sweet tea.

"Told you I was going to arrest you in front of your friends and everyone," the sheriff said with great satisfaction.

"I didn't kill Lexine," Franklin said.

"We'll talk about that back at the station," Sheriff Thompson replied as he peeled out of the parking lot and raced back toward Main Street.

Franklin sat back and banged his head against the seat. How could this be happening? He hadn't killed Lexine, any more than he'd killed Adrianna. Was the sheriff thinking he'd been too involved, like Charlene had been implying?

Mama would be so ashamed of him, right now. Sitting in the back of a police car! She might've closed the beauty salon for a week to hide her shame.

Since Franklin had recently been arrested, they didn't have to process him, like they normally would, with fingerprints and pictures. Instead, the sheriff took Franklin directly to an interview room. A camera, set up on a tripod, stared at him from the corner, the single eye of the lens accusing him of things he'd never even thought of doing. The chairs were hard and uncomfortable, the cushions made from black vinyl that squeaked every time Franklin shifted in his seat. A dingy, formerly white particleboard table sat between Franklin and the empty chair that would hold his interrogator.

Franklin had seen these rooms on so many TV shows. He'd sometimes wanted to be the one questioning the criminal, but he'd never wanted to be on this end of the table. The room felt small and closed in like a trap. He kept telling himself to take deep breaths, despite how stale the air smelled, how it felt like there wasn't enough of it.

Why were they making him wait like this? Franklin had assumed they'd just jump right into questioning or accusing him. Were they giving him time to stew? To think about his supposed crimes, so he'd be ready to confess to anything?

Franklin jumped when the door finally opened and the sheriff came in, carrying a plain file folder. He jumped again when the sheriff slapped it down on the table.

"I know we asked you these questions before, but I'm asking again. And this time, you better tell me the truth," the sheriff warned. "Where were you on Tuesday?"

"I was at work. You can check with anyone," Franklin said. At least Franklin knew he was covered there.

"And afterward?"

"I went home and worked in the field behind my house," Franklin said. He knew Lexine had been killed that afternoon, and he didn't have an alibi.

"And on your day off, Thursday, right? What did you do?" the sheriff asked.

"I worked around my farm," Franklin said. He shifted, then regretted it, as the vinyl squeaked.

"Break it down for me. Step by step," Sheriff Thompson said. His beady eyes bored deep into Franklin.

"I got up at my usual time—too damn early. Made breakfast, went out into the field back behind the house. Spent the day pulling weeds, tying up tomato plants, shoring up the chicken-wire fence the squash is climbing up," Franklin said smoothly. Those were all the things he'd actually done that day.

Darryl had always told Franklin to lie with as much truth as possible.

"Then how do you explain your fingerprints at Lexine's house?" the sheriff asked.

"She was my cousin? I saw her a lot?" Franklin pointed out reasonably. "I went out to her place often?"

"On one of the ears of corn placed next to her corpse?" Sheriff Thompson slipped a photo out of the folder.

There was that damn ear of corn, put there by Gloria. A white ruler had been photographed next to it. Franklin noted again that it had been growing well, before Gloria had ripped it off the stem.

"I didn't put that there," Franklin told the sheriff truthfully.

"Who did, then?" Sheriff Thompson said. He pointed to the corn. "You said there's no corn missing from your fields. But there are cobs missing from Karl Metzger's fields. You said you aren't stealing his corn. But here's a cob with your fingerprints on it. It was put there after Lexine and Earl Jackson were killed. Put there by you."

Franklin chuckled nervously and shook his head. "I swear to you, sheriff, I did not place that cob of corn there. I don't deny that it's from Karl's crop, or that my fingerprints are on it. But I did *not* put it there."

"I suppose you're going to tell me some damned creature dropped it there instead," the sheriff growled.

Franklin shrugged. "That's the honest truth, Sheriff. I swear. I didn't put it there. It was a ghost."

"How can you be so damn sure it was a ghost?" Sheriff Thompson asked, his eyes flicking from the photo to Franklin and back. "You've been guilty about something since the start. Were you there in the house?" When Franklin didn't reply, the sheriff slapped the table hard. "Answer me!"

Franklin jumped. He didn't want to admit that he'd been there, at the house. That just wouldn't be smart. Besides, Darryl would kill him if he confessed to anything.

"Stands to reason, don't it?" Franklin said reasonably. "I didn't put it there. Must have been a ghost. The ghost who took it from Karl's fields. Like she's been taking the rest of his crop."

"I don't believe in your ghosts. You put it there," the sheriff said, jamming his finger into the photo. "You were there. In the cabin. Before we arrived. And you didn't report the crime. Why?"

"I wasn't there," Franklin insisted. "And even if I had been there, I couldn't have reported the crime. There's no cell phone reception up at Lexine's place. It was one of the reasons why she bought that land."

"I know you were there," the sheriff said. "Or maybe, maybe you aren't lying about that. Maybe it's something else. Something you feel guilty about. Don't you want to tell me, Franklin?" Sheriff Thompson's tone turned more gentle. "Don't you want to help me get Lexine's killer?"

"I thought you said it was probably Earl Jackson," Franklin said. "I still think he killed her to bring the creature into being. He probably cast two spells, one while he was sitting in her driveway. Then he went and killed her, and it came."

"Why would he do a spell from her driveway?" the sheriff asked.

"You heard Eddie. She called it an abomination. Lexine wouldn't have helped Earl call it into being," Franklin explained reasonably.

"How did you know Earl called it from the driveway?" the sheriff said. "That his SUV was parked down at the far end of her property?"

Franklin felt himself grow still. His heart beat hard in his chest and his temple. "It just made sense," he said weakly.

"You were there," the sheriff said triumphantly. His tiny eyes glowed with satisfaction. "You *did* place that ear of corn next to Lexine. Maybe 'cause you were sorry you'd killed her."

Franklin sighed in exasperation and shook his head. "I keep telling you, I did *not* place that ear of corn next to her body." He looked away and took a deep breath. He could already hear Darryl yelling at him.

But Franklin just couldn't take it anymore.

"Hell with it. Was I there? Yes. I'd heard about the businessman missing, and I knew that Lexine could find him." Franklin took a deep breath. "But there's no *cell phone reception* at her property. I couldn't call the cops. Then I heard the sirens. So I took off. That's the truth." Cold chills ran up his spine, like a ghost had just appeared behind him.

Franklin didn't feel any relief for having told the sheriff, no weight lifted from his shoulders. Instead, he felt himself hunching up, closing off.

"I knew you weren't telling the truth," Sheriff Thompson said. "I knew you were there."

Franklin hung his head. He should have kept his mouth shut, like Darryl had told him to. Now, he was in even worse trouble than before.

"I'm gonna keep you here overnight," the sheriff explained. "So you can think about what you did, what you should have done."

"You already arrested me," Franklin pointed out, looking up. What was the sheriff going on about? Franklin already felt like shit.

"But we ain't charged you, yet." Sheriff Thompson sat back in his chair. "You'll be free to go in the morning."

"Why you keeping me here overnight?" Franklin asked. "What is it you want me to do here?"

"I don't want you to do anything," the sheriff admitted. "I just want you here."

"You think if I'm here, and y'all go after the creature tonight and just injure it, that I'll be safe here," Franklin said. "Too many people, cameras, and lights."

"Exactly," the sheriff said. "I knew you were smarter than you looked."

Franklin glared at the sheriff. No one but family got to say that kind of thing. "What about Darryl?"

"I've got men looking for him," the sheriff admitted. "But we haven't been able to find him. Would you know where he's at?"

Franklin shook his head. He was never admitting anything, ever again, to the sheriff. Even if the only reason he'd arrested Franklin was to keep him safe.

"Well, hopefully he'll be joining you soon. I'm not sure if we can get this thing, but I gotta try something." With that, the sheriff tapped the folder on the table once, twice, and stood up. "Anything else you'd care to tell me?"

"Don't do it," Franklin said. "Don't go after the creature like this. Y'all will either kill yourselves, or someone else."

"Either we're gonna stop this thing, or whatever it is, from killing more people," the sheriff said. "Or I'm gonna let you go and just use you for bait."

Franklin nodded. He'd expected nothing less.

CHAPTER 14

FRANKLIN SAT IN THE TINY cell just off the front room. He could still see the office from between the bars. The few remaining officers left until it was only him and the front clerk. The cell smelled like an office: burnt, cheap coffee; printer toner and too much paperwork; and a funny tangy smell that he finally recognized as gun oil. Cameras were trained on the cell from three different angles. The bars were cold, and weighed on his heart—they'd give him nightmares for years.

However, Franklin had to admit that a part of him was relieved. He'd be safe here. The creature—that thing of chaos and hate—wouldn't come here.

On the other hand, it *would* go seeking someone, and kill them, if the sheriff and his men were at all successful.

When an officer came in to speak with the desk sergeant, Franklin didn't heed him no mind, not until the pair of them approached his cell.

"Don't know why the sheriff's asking for him," the officer said with a shrug. "Just that I was to fetch him, right away." He wore his police hat down low on his forehead, and kept his face turned to one side.

The sergeant shook her head. "I don't like any of this," she said plainly. "I just don't." With a sigh, she swiped her card, then turned the key in the lock. "You need to go with this officer," she said resignedly.

Franklin wondered what had gone wrong. Why did the sheriff need him? Had someone already been killed? He held his tongue until they reached the front street.

Instead of a police cruiser, he saw Darryl's big black truck.

Only then did Franklin look closely at the officer holding his arm so tightly. "Darryl?" he whispered urgently. "What the hell are you doing?"

"Breaking you out of jail," Darryl said with a grin.

Franklin couldn't help but gasp. Breaking someone out of a holding cell had to be a felony. Along with impersonating an officer. Shit, they were in it now.

"Wait," Franklin said, stopping in the middle of the broad sidewalk.

"We can't," Darryl said, tugging on him. "You never know when that desk sergeant'll catch a clue. We gotta go! Now!"

"The sheriff is gonna lock us both up and throw away the key," Franklin complained, but he let himself be tugged along. "Goddamn it. We're never gonna hear the end of this one." He climbed into the passenger side of the cab.

"Sheriff'll forgive us, once we get the creature," Darryl told Franklin as they raced down Main Street, hanging a hard left, heading toward the highway.

"And how we gonna do that?" Franklin asked. He was gonna lose the farm. What kind of ghosts would visit him in prison? He shivered.

"Well, you love your corn, right? And I love hunting. Between the pair of us, we'll have enough love to slaughter it," Darryl reasoned.

Traffic out of town was light. Still, Darryl gunned his engine and honked his horn when an old car just sat at the first stoplight, not moving after it turned green. "Stupid farmhand," he muttered as he raced by.

Franklin stayed quiet. He couldn't imagine the trouble they were in. Mama would have his hide for something like this.

But he also didn't see any other way. He needed to be out in his field when the creature came calling.

Darryl spun gravel as he slid into Franklin's driveway. He had his door open just as the truck came to a stop.

But Franklin grabbed Darryl's arm before he could get out. "No," he said firmly.

"No? What the hell are you going on about?" Darryl asked.

"You're not going with," Franklin told his cousin. "It's me. And my fields. You're going home to your family, Darryl."

"You're my family too," Darryl pointed out.

"All right, then, to your wife and kids. You don't love hunting. Would you give it up if your youngest, Tommy, got hurt, and needed you?"

"That's not fair," Darryl said.

"Would you?" Franklin insisted.

Darryl slowly nodded. "Of course. He's my boy," he said with a shrug.

"That's why it's gotta be me," Franklin said. "Me, and my fields, and my love of sweet popping corn." Nothing else made sense to him.

"Now you're the one's gonna get himself killed," Darryl complained.

"No, I ain't," Franklin said. "Go home. Get yourself an alibi, one that'll hold up in court. I'm gonna go fight that beast. Kill it with love."

"Cuz—you don't have to do this by yourself," Darryl said. "We all know how brave you are. We seen it all summer."

Mama and Gloria appeared next to the house, on the walk leading around to the fields out back.

"I won't be alone," Franklin assured Darryl.

FRANKLIN STEPPED out of Darryl's truck into the cooling night air. With a final wave, Darryl pulled out of the driveway, spitting gravel as he raced away, leaving Franklin alone with his ghosts.

The farm house stood like a dark shadow, cut off from the rest of the living night. The cycling cicada song returned, louder than ever. Clouds hung over the sky, reflecting back the lights from town with a weird orange glow.

Sweet Bess appeared next to the house, before ambling off into the fields. Franklin shivered, a chill spreading across his back, as if a whole platoon of ghosts had just arrived, that he couldn't see. Franklin took one last deep breath, then turned toward Mama and Gloria.

Worry poured out from both ghosts. They knew what he was planning to do. "Mama, it'll be okay," Franklin reassured her as he walked past, toward his field. "We can fight this thing. And win."

Franklin didn't have to see their expressions to know they glared at him. But there wasn't anything he could do about that.

With one last look up toward the stars, Franklin stepped across the first row of corn, pushing past the stalks. Instantly, the cries of the cicadas cycled up, their sound deafening. Leaves rustled all around Franklin, like a quiet summer promise. The smell of good black dirt rose up to greet him.

Mama and Gloria appeared on either side of Franklin, then they passed forward, into the next row of corn. Franklin followed them into the very heart of the field.

Mama came to stand next to Franklin, then held out her hands toward one of his ears of corn.

Franklin stifled his own cry when one of the perfect cobs fell, yet one more victim of the creature.

Mama *shoved* the fallen soldier with her will, rolling it right to Franklin's feet. With a sigh, he bent to pick it up. It felt heavy in his hands, weighty with purpose.

He hoped it was enough.

Peeling back the husk just a tiny bit, Franklin admired the formidably straight rows of kernels. He didn't strip the husk from the ear to see for certain, but maybe this would have been an ear he could have entered into the "most perfect cob" category of the State Fair.

Now, he'd use it as a weapon. He built up his admiration for this perfect cob. Bringing it close to his nose, he smelled the sweetness of the kernels, felt the summer heat still captured in its rows.

Cold struck Franklin, as if someone had just opened the deep freeze at the grocery store. The creature whirled into being, just a few feet away. It casually made space for itself, cutting down half a dozen stalks.

Franklin seethed as he stared at the creature. He'd never be able to love this whirling mass of chaos. It was the opposite of everything he did love, the neat rows of his field, the order of the seasons. "You will leave," Franklin said, holding out his single ear of corn, as if it were an old-time sword. "You will leave this earth and never return."

The creature whirled in place, contemplating. It struck out suddenly with one of its whip-like arms, aiming to knock the cob from Franklin's hand.

Franklin struck back. He blocked the creature's attack, forcing the arm away.

He stepped back, surprised. How had he done that? He looked at the cob of corn in his hands with amazement and awe.

Love it was.

When the creature struck out again, Franklin was ready, and he slashed the cob of corn in front of him, keeping the creature's spikes off his body.

His wonderful, beautiful, *perfect* corn could do this. He knew that it had the power to win the State Fair this year. His corn was better than any Karl could grow.

Step by step, Franklin drove the creature back, out of the center of the field, toward the road. Maybe it could get caught up in the trees and blackberry brambles lining the lane.

Mama appeared next to Franklin, her arms crossed over her ample chest. Pride radiated from her.

Franklin, her boy, was finally doing good.

Gloria, too, appeared. Her impatience spilled out into the night. She wanted Franklin to finish this creature. *Now.* Before it went back to Karl and his fields and destroying everything else.

Bolstered by his ladies, Franklin took a broad step forward, pushing the creature back. Off his property. Out of his field. Out of this world.

The creature gathered itself up and attacked again. But it chose a different target this time.

It attacked Mama.

"No!" Franklin cried as the thing tore into Mama's ghost. He struck out at its whips with his cob of corn.

The cob broke in two, sliced cleanly through by the thing's whips.

"Crap!" Franklin said, stepping back.

The thing continued to tear into Mama. White bits of ghost floated through the air. The thing's intent was clear: It planned on tearing Mama apart.

A white flash raced by Franklin, slamming into the creature.

Gloria.

The creature let go of Mama in surprise, and she disappeared. Gloria gave her impressive silent scream as she beat at the creature with fists that couldn't land a punch. However, the creature paused in the face of such passion.

But even the force of Gloria's emotion wouldn't stop it for long.

Franklin pulled off another cob. He told himself hurriedly that it was still perfect in every way. He imagined what it would have tasted like, once it had been properly dried. Would each kernel have the proper legs? Enough crunch, but not too much? He'd never know, now.

When the creature lashed out at Franklin, he repelled it again. But this time, the thing held its ground. Franklin couldn't force it back further.

Mama reappeared beside her boy. When the creature switched targets, Mama rebuked it, pushing away its whips with her hands. She couldn't attack it, but it could no longer attack her.

When Franklin glanced over, he saw that Mama now carried a photo of Papa, nestled in her bosom.

With renewed vigor, Franklin and Mama attacked the creature, now on opposite sides of it. They were intent, both of them, on driving it off.

Gloria also pushed at the thing. But her passion merely fed it. Whenever she got closer and gave her silent scream, it spun faster, and its attacks grew harder.

Franklin's arms grew tired of battling. His heart was full. He could love, oh, he could love.

But while his soul was willing, his flesh was weakening.

"Gloria!" Franklin cried. "Would you go make yourself useful somewhere else?"

Franklin only felt relief when she disappeared again. But it was short-lived. The creature attacked again, sharper and harder. Franklin lost one cob, then another. He grabbed wildly for yet another, pulling it off a stalk without looking.

It was a runt, smaller than the others.

Still, Franklin had a desperate love for it, even this one. It would never be perfect, but neither had he been. Despite that, his life was still full of surprising joy, of love and care that popped up whenever he needed it most.

Franklin struck out again, his muscles aching, his hand sweaty, and his grip slipping. But he had to keep going. This thing could *not* win.

"Holy shit," someone said behind Franklin.

"Karl?" Franklin asked, surprised. "What the hell are you doing here?" Franklin struck out at the creature, forcing away the whip that had reached for Karl. Mama engaged the creature again, making it turn toward her for a few moments, giving Franklin a bit of breathing room.

"I just...the sheriff, and his men, were shooting up my field. And somehow, I knew, I *knew* I should come see how you were doing. What the hell is that thing?" Karl asked.

"You can see it?" Franklin asked, surprised. "It's the creature that's been living in your fields. That thing that's been attacking folks. It's what Gloria's been trying to protect you from. I've been trying to drive it off."

"With this?" Karl asked, gesturing toward Franklin's runt of a cob.

"It's been working so far!" Franklin said, annoyed as he thwacked the creature again.

An ear of corn appeared at Karl's feet. When Franklin looked up, Gloria stood there. "I think that's from your fields," Franklin guessed.

Gloria nodded.

"What am I supposed to do with it?" Karl asked, dumbfounded.

"Pick it up, idiot! Fight!" Franklin directed.

The thing surged forward again, trying to get at Karl.

Franklin wasn't about to let that happen. He might envy Karl— Hell, he might've wanted to *be* Karl at one point—but this thing wasn't gonna hurt his competitor.

What had Karl said? That Franklin made him a better man, making him try harder?

Shit. Karl had done the same for Franklin.

Without hesitation, Franklin attacked the creature, defending Karl.

The thing lashed out with all its fury and strength, aiming to destroy Franklin, his field, all he loved. It struck Mama, Gloria, the stalks of his beloved corn.

Franklin cried out when one of the creature's whips ripped across his side. The pain hurt worse than when Mama had died. He staggered to the left, his hand coming away bloody.

Karl surged forward. "No!" he commanded. He struck out with his own cob of corn, beating the thing back before it could press its advantage.

Franklin took a breath, then another. Pain bit into him. He told himself it was nothing, like he'd just been riding up College Hill and had a stitch in his side. He could do this.

Karl wasn't as skilled with his cob—or maybe he didn't love his corn as much as Franklin. He was already in trouble, the thing gaining.

Franklin pushed himself back into the fight, racing around the thing, attacking it from behind, drawing it away from Karl.

It wasn't that he loved Karl, no. That would've been too much to ask. But Karl represented everything Franklin wanted to be, that perfect farmer who made his living from his fields, independent and proud.

With both of them attacking, one on either side, the thing didn't know where to go. It lashed out first at Franklin, then at Karl, but it couldn't get through.

Then Mama joined Franklin on his right side, and Gloria on his left, boxing the thing in.

The thing didn't know where to go. If it attacked any of them, the others closed in. Even Karl realized they weren't alone. "There's other ghosts here, aren't there?" he asked as Mama and Gloria took turns pushing at the thing.

"Gloria's here, yeah." Franklin didn't want to admit Mama was there as well—didn't think that was any of Karl's business.

"Thank them for me, would you?" Karl said after taking another deep breath and diving into the fight again.

All together, they pressed in, containing the creature, draining away the fury of its attack. It whirled more slowly now, its advantage becoming its weakness. It didn't have any room. Its attacks were shortened, slower.

Franklin panted, his arms tired, his legs trembling with the effort. Hell, even his *will* hurt, forcing the creature away, diminishing the thing, making it fold in on itself.

It had no place here, though, not in Katherinesville, not in her fields or woods, not in her hills or lowlands, not even in the hearts of the people who got angry or hateful.

As purple fingers of dawn stretched across the sky, the thing finally collapsed in on itself. It stopped whirling, changing from a dust devil into a small cloud, the size of a basketball. Its color cleared too, growing to a cleaner white.

Was this what Earl Jackson had originally tried to raise? Something less evil, more of a familiar?

It still had the chance to grow back, though. With one last blow, Franklin cleaved it in two, breaking the heart of it.

With a sigh that could even be heard over the chorus of cicadas, the thing flowed out over the ground, like morning fog, fading away into the good solid earth.

Franklin wiped the sweat away from his brow with the back of his arm. Karl, standing across the way, looked rough: A line of blood ran along his jaw, from where the creature had tagged him. His arms were bleeding, too, and as he walked forward, he limped badly, barely able to put any weight on his right leg.

Gloria stepped in front of Karl. For a moment, she flared, bright and white.

Karl's eyes opened wide and he gasped. "Gloria?" he asked.

Her *intent* spilled across the empty field. *Next time, actually ask the girl out.*

"Yes, ma'am. I will," Karl fervently promised.

Then she was gone.

Mama beamed proudly at Franklin.

He knew he looked a mess, bleeding from his side, his arm, who knew how many other places. He could barely draw a breath, and his legs felt like they was made out of jelly.

Still, Mama was proud of her boy. Franklin felt her love flow around him. Her absolute conviction that he was gonna be all right now, *finally*, washed over him as she faded.

Papa's photo floated down from where she'd been standing.

Franklin groaned as he reached down to pick it up. Damn, he hurt.

Karl gave a low whistle. "Your field's ruined," he said softly. "I'm sorry for that."

Franklin nodded. All his stalks had been knocked over—either by the creature, or by them, fighting it. He'd known that would happen, going in.

It was a sacrifice he'd been willing to make.

"Think we need the emergency room?" Franklin asked, offering his arm for Karl to lean against as they started trudging out of the field, stepping over the fallen stalks, toward the house.

"Either that or the psych ward," Karl said. "Shit. I still don't rightly believe what just went on."

Franklin shrugged. He was used to that.

As they reached the house, Sheriff Thompson pulled up in his Crown Vic, the lights flashing. He marched over to Franklin.

"Franklin Kanly, I—" The sheriff stopped, blinking. "What the hell happened to you two?"

"What do you think, sheriff?" Karl asked belligerently. "We finally decided to settle the score with each other."

The sheriff just grunted. "So you was the one who broke him out of jail."

Karl shrugged. "No. And you'll never prove it."

"All right. Let's get you both to the hospital," the sheriff said. He looked out over Franklin's fields. "All your popping corn's gone, ain't it?"

Franklin nodded.

"And whatever thing that's been plaguing us, it's gone too?" Sheriff Thompson asked, still looking out over the fields.

"Yes, sir, it is," Franklin said firmly.

The sheriff nodded, still staring at the fields. "Might just have been a misunderstanding at the judicial center," he said slowly. "Accidentally releasing you early. Since you weren't gonna be charged with anything."

"Thank you, sir," Franklin said.

"But if anything like this ever happens again," the sheriff said, his beady eyes boring into Franklin, "you're gonna be the first one I'm coming after."

"Understood," Franklin said, too tired to feel much threatened.

The sheriff looked over at Karl. "So, the story's going to be that you beat each other within an inch of your lives, isn't it. Feel better now?"

Franklin and Karl looked at each other. Franklin couldn't help his grin. "We'll make each other better men yet, sir."

"Who knows?" Karl asked as they shuffled to the sheriff's car. "Might even go into business together."

"Selling popping corn?" Franklin asked.

"What else?" Karl said. "We'd make a hell of a team."

Franklin agreed. They'd still be competing, trying to top each other with better ideas and products.

But even if they didn't make a go of it, Mama was still right.

Franklin was gonna be okay, now.

ABOUT THE AUTHOR

Leah Cutter writes page-turning fiction in exotic locations, such as a magical New Orleans, the ancient Orient, Hungary, the Oregon coast, rural Kentucky, Seattle, Minneapolis, and many others.

She writes literary, fantasy, mystery, science fiction, and horror fiction. Her short fiction has been published in magazines like *Alfred Hitchcock's Mystery Magazine* and *Talebones*, anthologies like Fiction River, and on the web. Her long fiction has been published both by New York publishers as well as small presses.

Find Leah's books here.

Follow her blog at www.LeahCutter.com.

Reviews

It's true. Reviews help me sell more books. If you've enjoyed this story, please consider leaving a review of it on your favorite site.

Come someplace new...

Are you a traveler? Do you enjoy exploring strange new worlds, new cultures, new people?

Sign up for my newsletter and I'll start you on your travels with a free copy of my book, *The Island Sampler*.

I will never spam you or use your email for nefarious purposes. You can also unsubscribe at any time.

http://www.LeahCutter.com/newsletter/

ABOUT BOOK VIEW CAFÉ

Book View Café is a professional authors' cooperative offering DRM-free ebooks in multiple formats to readers around the world. With authors in a variety of genres including mystery, romance, fantasy, and science fiction, Book View Café has something for everyone.

Book View Café is good for readers because you can enjoy high-quality DRM-free ebooks from your favorite authors at a reasonable price.

Book View Café is good for writers because 95% of the profit goes directly to the book's author.

Book View Café authors include Nebula, Hugo, and Philip K. Dick Award winners, Nebula, Hugo, World Fantasy, and Rita Award nominees, and *New York Times* bestsellers and notable book authors.

www.bookviewcafe.com